the exception

Three Player Grind Book 4

allyson lindt

acelette press

To everyone who has sacrificed pieces of themselves for the ones they love.

1
kandace

I DIDN'T RECOGNIZE MYSELF.

The woman reflected back at me in the shop window in Milan wore my face. Her blond hair was pulled into the same tight bun I'd styled my own hair in a few hours ago, and her violet dress was both elegant and understated, like the one I'd put on earlier tonight.

But the man at her side, the one more than a decade younger than my forty-five, with tattoos peeking above the collar of his shirt, and obvious where he'd rolled up his sleeves, looked more like he should be working for my brother's old company than showing me fountains in the middle of the night.

As in, my brother's internet porn company, second largest in the world, that he'd sold a few years ago.

Joystick even had a name like an adult film star.

"You okay?" he asked, his hand coming to rest at the small of my back.

I shook the random thought aside and yanked my gaze from our reflection. Maybe I had stepped into someone else's life for the night, and I was going to enjoy the heck out of it. "I'm fantastic."

"Good." Joystick nudged me toward a looming iron gate, held up by tall stone pillars. "This is the place I was talking about. It's beautiful this time of year. The summer flowers have faded, but there are fall blooms and the colors of the leaves... You have to see for yourself."

Yes, my possible-porn-God wanted to show me a garden. At night. In Italy. The man who, for all I knew, actually was a cam-boy. I'd just met him tonight, at the pre-grand opening for a restaurant I was financing. He was friends with the owners, and I trusted their business sense enough to give them millions of my dollars.

That didn't mean I knew anything about their taste in people, but they adored one of my favorite employees, and that spoke highly of them.

So the stranger I was strolling into a park with at ten at night was probably not dangerous.

Though the wicked, who-am-I part of me, the part who loved my racing pulse and the way my heart beat faster every time Joystick brushed a hand over my arm or back, hoped at least a little of him was.

He slipped his hand around mine, and there was the skip of my heart again. We strolled through the front gates.

Flowers and exotic grasses and trees lined the

cobblestone pathways, vibrant even in the darkness. The soft scents drifted to tease us and wrap around us. There was no one else here, not this late, and it was like we'd stepped into a fantasy realm.

It was stunning.

I couldn't think of anything to say beyond that, so I stopped in front of a neatly trimmed bush of wild roses. "The colors are so vibrant." I cupped one of the blooms, careful to not touch the petals.

"That which we call a rose by any other name would smell as sweet."

It wasn't the Shakespeare that caught me off-guard, it was that he knew more of the quote than most people. I turned to Joystick. "Did you just quote Romeo and Juliet at me?"

"Habit." He shrugged. "I had those lines drilled into my head so much when... Weird, I know." He grinned.

Wait. "When what?"

"When I played Romeo?"

Like, in a school play? In a porn? I studied him, which seemed odd, because I'd been staring at bits of him most of the night. But now I was looking at his face. "Oh." Realization spread through me. "*Oh.*" He meant when he played Romeo in the modern adaptation that came out years ago. "You're... *oh.* That's why you look familiar. My son loved your show when it was in syndication." I was standing in front of a teen movie star, but all grown up.

Was it weird that I'd been lusting after him all

night? It wasn't as though he was any younger now than when I met him, and it wasn't like I ever looked at him on TV and said *I'd tap that*.

Joystick smirked. "Wait. Who did you think I was?"

"It doesn't matter." I turned my attention back to the flowers. At least the darkness would hide any blush associated with the heat flooding my cheeks.

"No. It matters. Who did you think I was?" His tone was playful rather than insistent.

I strolled farther down the path, trying to focus on the stunning blooms around us. "Someone else."

Joystick caught up to me, grabbed my wrist loosely, and spun me to face him. "I'm going to keep asking. It's about me. I think it's fair I know."

"My brother founded Smut Central." I hated throwing around that name, or even looking like I was dropping it. Andrew sold a few years back, but the original site had been his brainchild.

Joystick's mouth formed an *O*, but no sound came out. And then he barked a laugh. "Fuck me. You thought I was a professional fucker?"

"You looked familiar, and with the body, and the tattoos, and— I'm gonna stop now."

"Don't stop on my account. Feel free to keep telling me how I look like I do porn."

I hid my face. "I think what I should do instead is get back to my hotel." Stepping out of my comfort zone was a mistake, and now I'd humiliated myself.

"No." He grabbed my wrist again, and a shock of

want raced through me. "Rather, you can if you want, but don't do it because of that. I'd much rather you thought…" A wince passed over Joystick's face and vanished in a blink. "If I promise I fuck a lot better than a porn star, will you stay?"

"I've never been with a porn star, so I don't have a bar for what that means." Oh. My. God. Did I just say that?

He tugged me down the path, further into the park. "I promise it means good things. But if you want, we can forget we ever had this conversation."

"I'd very much like that." It couldn't possibly be so simple. I'd just told him he looked like a guy who had sex on camera for a living, and he not only preferred that to the truth, but was willing to pretend I hadn't said it.

What kind of guy did both?

"These over here are one of my favorites." Joystick led us toward some orange flowers that looked like tiny, heart-shaped balloons. "Someone told me they're called winter cherries. And these"—he gestured toward some that were like red platters with… tiny green penises—"are anthurium, and not dick plates like I originally thought."

He was really willing to make light of this. Okay, I could stick around for this kind of tour.

As we walked, he continued to point out some of his favorites, and as the path looped back around to the entrance, disappointment crept up inside that the walk was almost over.

"Uh, fuck." His exclamation caught me off-guard.

My gaze landed on the now-closed gates. *Oh.* Yeah, that warranted his reaction.

He whistled sharply, followed by a loud shout of, "*Hello,*" echoing in the night.

There was no answer.

A sign on the back of the wrought-iron caught my attention. *I Cancelled Chiudono Alle 11.* I had no idea what that meant, except that the English text underneath said *Gates Close at 11.*

Well, crap. "Joystick." I pointed.

"Ah." He let out a sheepish laugh—because this sexy as hell man could also look sheepish apparently and that made him sexier—and rubbed the back of his head. "Oops. I guess I've never been here this late before."

This was why I didn't take risks. Why I followed the rules and was responsible. Why I didn't leave dinner parties with strange, tattooed men.

So why couldn't I find it in me to be upset? "What now?" I was asking myself as much as him. "Is there a number we can call? Do we shout louder?"

"There's a shorter fence over there." Joystick gestured. "We'll climb out."

I stared at him in disbelief.

"What?" He asked.

I gestured down at my gown, which would be brushing the ground if it weren't for the short heels I wore. "I'm not exactly dressed for climbing fences."

"It's only three or four feet tall. I'll help."

It seemed smarter to me to make a better plan, which both of mine were. When he grabbed my hand again, my brain short-circuited at the warmth of his grip. Because apparently I was a silly little girl who couldn't control herself around a pretty man.

Joystick tugged along a narrow path, through a wide enough section of plants that none of them caught my dress, toward a much shorter iron fence that ran around the property.

"I can't climb that." I looked between it and him with disbelief.

"Easier than it looks, I promise. It's just like stepping into a tall truck."

Talk about impractical. "Which I also avoid whenever possible."

Joystick chuckled. "It works like this. Use me and the stone support to steady yourself, and step into my hands." He interlocked his fingers and held them down like a sling. "Then step on the stone support and hop down onto the grass at the other side."

"Your confidence in my skill is sweet, but I can't."

He hovered his mouth near my ear, his warm breath teasing my skin. "You can."

Was he right? It was only three or four feet. I couldn't, could I? Maybe I could. "Okay."

I swore my entire body was shaking as I steadied myself on the short pillar and his shoulder, and placed my foot in his hands. But as I found my balance, I grew more confident.

Between Joystick and the pillar, my weight was

supported. He helped me move higher, so I could step onto the top of the stone without much reach.

Placing my foot on the rocky structure, I pushed up enough to clear the iron fence. I could do this.

My foot slipped on the stone. My world twisted and spun. I tried to push off, to minimize damage. It didn't matter, I was falling.

I landed on the grass on my back, a grunt escaping my chest along with all the air in my lungs. Were those cartoon birds dancing in front of my eyes?

"Kandace." Joystick sounded so worried.

Out of the corner of my eye I saw him vault the fence in a single leap, and land by my side. Because of course he was capable of that. I was flat on my back, in the middle of nowhere in a foreign country, and a fence-vaulting, tattooed hottie was kneeling next to me, asking if I was hurt.

This was so ludicrous it might as well be straight out of its own bad movie.

The thought bubbled up inside me, carried on amusement, and I laughed. I couldn't stop. The laughter was pouring out in peals, tears stinging my eyelids, and I was still going.

"Kandace?" Joystick looked concerned, but he was also laughing. "Come on." He offered me a hand.

Silliness overtook me, and rather than letting him help me up, I tugged him down. He lost his balance and then he was falling too, to land straddling my waist, hands on either side of my head.

He did that on purpose.

I didn't care. He was staring at me with bright blue eyes surrounded by dark lashes and pale skin and for the second time in as many minutes, my breath left me.

"You're even more stunning when you let go." Joystick's voice was gravel, and his heat surrounded me in an all-encompassing blanket that blocked out the rest of the world.

I had no idea what to say to a comment like that. "Thank you." My reply came out shyly.

Who was I?

"If I promise to show you a good time, and *not* fuck you like a porn star, will you come back to my room with me?" Joystick asked.

I knew he hadn't actually let it go, but I wasn't sure I cared. "I'd have to take your word for it."

He leaned in until his mouth was millimeters from mine. "Trust me, you'll know," he whispered.

Oh. My.

"Okay," I said.

His smirk did delicious things to my insides. He grabbed my hand, and this time I let him tug me to my feet. After spending far longer than was probably necessary with him brushing grass off the back of my dress, he wrapped an arm around my waist, and led me back to the streets.

Tomorrow I'd go back to being good, boring Kandace. Tonight, I was going to let the tattooed hottie with the ridiculous name and the smokin' body make good on his promises.

2
kandace

JOYSTICK'S HOTEL was simple and understated, but clean and quiet. I was surprised we weren't stepping into some sort of overstated opulence, but also grateful. I had money now, though I'd come from very little, and the journey tended to mean more to me than how one flashed their cash once they had it.

As he let us into his room, my heart was hammering so loudly in my chest, I didn't know how I heard anything else. Could he hear that *bam bam bam* from behind my ribs?

He cupped my face between his palms with a touch that was so gentle it ached, and drew his thumb along my bottom lip.

I wasn't a forty-five-year-old virgin, or anything so comedy movie cliche, but I hadn't been with many men in my life, and most of those experiences had been... *lacking*. The desire that raced through me now was as intoxicating as wine. Terrifying and incredible.

"The moment you walked into the restaurant tonight, I was fantasizing about stripping you out of this dress." Joystick's voice was deep and seductive and rolled over my skin.

What was I supposed to do with a comment like that? Be offended? Turned on?

I was definitely more of the latter. I wanted his touch to move beyond my face. Or even a kiss would be nice.

"Let me show you the night of your life, in orgasms," he said.

That wasn't a high bar, based on my past, but I wasn't going to tell him that. "That's a big promise."

"Good. I'm an overachiever. May I fuck you?"

Wow that was quite a question. Possibly the hottest one I'd ever been asked. "Yes."

He dipped his head and brushed his mouth over mine. Finally. His lips were soft with that first touch, but turned hard and demanding in a blink, stealing my breath. His tongue was rough, his grip rougher as he captured my neck and devoured my whimpers.

If this was how he opened, I may not survive the intensity of the night. But I'd die happy, with a stupid 'ol grin on my face.

Joystick spun me away from him with an effortless twirl, but I swore his mouth never left me, gliding along my jaw, down my neck, and to bathe my shoulders in attention. He dragged down the zipper of my dress, and let the fabric fall away.

He pressed into my back, his clothing rough and

tantalizing against my bare skin. Each new touch from him kept me from thinking too much. Kept the self-consciousness at bay.

My bra fell away as easily as my dress, leaving me in panties and heels, in the middle of a stranger's room, while he covered my neck and shoulders with kisses and playfully hungry nips.

Joystick's low groan rumbled through my back as he slid his palms up my stomach. He caught my earlobe between his teeth and tugged. "You're way hotter than I imagined."

His words heated my skin as much as his touch. Did I say *thank you* to a comment like that? When he cupped my breasts, I let a moan be my reply. It was far easier than thinking. Especially when he moved his mouth back to my neck and sucked hard enough to leave a sting.

He rolled my nipples between his fingers, and the way he worked the tender skin where my neck met my shoulder, he was going to leave one hell of a hickey.

The need between my legs pulsed harder. More intensely. I tried to squeeze my thighs together to hold it back, but that just made me more aware of how much his touch was driving me wild.

"What do you like in the bedroom, Kandace?" Joystick scraped his teeth over my skin.

I had no idea. "I was promised orgasms."

"And you'll get them." His chuckle was tasty. "I

was looking for more of an idea of how you'd like to get there."

If he kept doing what he was doing, I'd be a puddle of pleasure soon enough, but I had a feeling he meant to add more to the experience. "Surprise me?" I said. We were already past the point of wham-bam-thank-you-ma'am that I expected from a fling.

"Stop me if you don't like something."

Before I could process his words, he slipped his hand into the back elastic of my panties, and yanked up hard, wedging them into place.

That was awkward. But also, the way the tight fabric pressed into my core intensified my arousal.

When his palm landed flat and hard against my behind, and a loud *smack* filled the room, I was double surprised, and my groan escaped before my brain could catch up.

"You like that?" He asked.

I nodded. "Yes."

He glided his hands down my arms, and placed my palms against the wall. And then he slapped the other ass cheek. He alternated, back and forth, pausing every few smacks to run his touch along my stinging skin. There was no rhythm to it, so each new impact was a surprise.

He kept going until my behind was numb. When he pressed his leg into one side of me, as he rubbed the other cheek, the contrasting sensations short circuited my thoughts.

"You're as bright red as those wild roses." He

moved his hand to my breastbone and pulled me into him again. "But far more fucking gorgeous."

If any more heat flooded through me, my skin might ignite.

Joystick slipped lower, his touch trailing over my stomach and past my waist, to the cord of wadded up cotton between my legs.

I'd already soaked through the panties. The way he pressed them into me mingled with the lingering sting of the spanking, plus desperation spilling from me. He teased and coaxed until my hips were working without my permission.

Every bit of this was incredible, but if the goal was orgasms, this wasn't doing it.

When Joystick pushed the last of my clothing to the ground, the fabric clung to me before finally pulling away. Those were wrecked.

I didn't care.

And when he pressed his fingers to my swollen clit, nothing else in the world mattered. I was so worked up that it didn't take much for him to make me come. Orgasm flooded me, and I gripped his arm tightly, leaning against him as my legs threatened to give out.

He eased away as the pleasure ebbed, and kissed the edge of my arm. "Now that you're warmed up…"

Did I want him to finish that thought?

"Hmm." His consideration joined the hum buzzing under my skin. "I'd love to press you to the balcony glass and let Milan watch while I fuck you."

Oh, Christ. I loved the idea as much as I hated it. A *yes* bubbled up in my throat. "Not tonight."

Damn it, responsible me, where did you come from? Did I just ruin the night? Would this be where he told me to get my clothes and get out?

"Okay," Joystick said.

Like that, this man was that much hotter.

"Do you want to stop?" he asked.

"No." Definitely not. Please, no.

"Thank fuck." His touch fell away, and he moved to stand in front of me. "Sit on the bed."

Okay?

Now I had time to think, and that might not be a good thing. I was sitting naked in a stranger's room, after one hell of an orgasm. If I were by myself, I'd be done for the night and either go to sleep or more likely go get more work done.

But he was stripping out of his clothing.

The view was incredible. Ink snaked along his arms and chest, covering and enhancing a well-toned body. I couldn't believe *he* wanted *me*.

And when he pushed off the last of his clothes, when his cock sprung free, I had to snap my jaw shut to keep from gawking. A bar with two metal balls, one on each end, pierced the tip of his dick.

"Oh." My surprise slipped out anyway, and I didn't realize I was reaching for him, until he covered my hand with his.

"You like it?" He drew my touch closer.

Did I? I'd never seen... Especially not in person. I

ran my touch up his shaft and over the metal bar, and he jerked against my hand. His drawn-out groan had my body humming even louder in anticipation. "Does it hurt?"

"Not normally. But it will feel really good for both of us if it's used right."

Used right? There weren't a lot of ways to use a penis, but he sounded like he knew what he was doing. It was almost a disappointment to see him roll on a condom, but I could still see the tempting little bar through the thin rubber.

Joystick placed his hands on the mattress, next to my hips, and pressed his lips to mine as he nudged my body back with his. At the prompting, I scooted further up on the bed, trying not to break the contact between us in the process. Everywhere his skin met mine there were sparks.

And then I was lying down, with him hovering over me. This was like in the park, but with no clothes between us. I couldn't help but study him further, tracing my fingers along his tattoos. Especially the more vibrant colors.

The soft moans he made, the way he sucked in sharp breaths when I touched certain spots, filled me with a new kind of temptation. I had power here after all, even boxed underneath this imposing, playful man.

He teased the head of his cock along my slit, and a shock of pleasure jarred me each time that metal ball bumped my clit. In retaliation, I dragged a thumb over his nipple… my nails up his sides… tilted my head up to lick up his chest… and loved the way his expression shifted through ranges of enjoyment with each new touch.

Joystick fell closer, startling me, and crushed his mouth to mine. "Enough play." His growl was rough and enticing.

The rest of the world fell away when he thrust inside me. I was so turned on, he slid in easily, but he was big enough to stretch me out. And I felt when he struck deep inside. Felt that piercing hit just the right spot when he straightened his body, driving him deeper.

He sought out my clit again, and the sensations inside me, combined with him pressing his thumb into me, were almost too much. I hovered on a thread between uncomfortable and the promise of bliss.

"Let go." Joystick's words were as much encouragement as command. "Just let this overtake you."

I didn't know if I could. But I wanted to. I needed to. I—

Christ.

Climax spilled through me, filling me past the brink. As I hit the peak, Joystick started pounding hard and fast. Frantic.

I didn't know where I stopped and he began. I didn't care. I clenched around him, I needed to keep him in me. There were so many sensations… I'd never felt this. I was floating on a cloud of intensity.

The sounds he made when he came were primal

and delicious. The way he tensed. His grip digging into my thighs.

We were floating away. So far away.

The edges of reality fuzzed back in as he slowed to a stop, but we were still in our own little world. He dropped his head between my breasts, his skin hot against mine, as we both caught our breath.

And when Joystick rolled to my side, he grabbed me and pulled me with him, as he fell out of me. "That was fun. In the most amazing way," he said.

I was glad it wasn't just good for me. "It really was."

"Thank you for being my best night in Italy, Kandace." He kissed me on the nose, on the chin, and on the lips.

Was I grinning like a dork? I assumed. "Thank you for setting the bar impossibly high for anyone in the future, Joystick." I shouldn't have said that out loud.

I didn't care.

"You're quite welcome."

I was never doing something like this again. Tomorrow I'd go back to my ordered, responsible life. But I had no regrets about tonight. It would be an incredible memory, and that was all I needed.

Tomorrow I'd go back to being responsible. Tonight, I was going to linger in this fantasy.

3
elijah

NOTHING in the world compared to the excited buzz that hung in the air on set during the first days of shooting a new movie.

As a teenager, I thought I needed to be one of the stars to appreciate this high. When I lost that chance, when I made the mistake of fucking *the* star, and the decision fucked me in return, I thought I'd lost this feeling forever.

"Eli, hey," one of the Assistant Directors called from across the large warehouse where they were setting up. "If you're here before we even start, should I be worried?"

"Nah." I waved Alvin off. "Everything's amicable." I understood his concern. These days I was a script fixer, rather than an actor. And I wasn't typically on set unless the producers expected to need a *lot* of fixing, right now. Typically because they disagreed with the original writers.

This time, Writer, Director, and Producer were all the same guy. Everyone thought a portion of their life would make a good movie, but in Andrew's case he was probably right. He'd backpacked around the world after high school, and started one of the biggest internet porn companies in the world in the process. I was pretty sure no one else could say both. Plus his whole story was tied off with the gorgeous bow of *and then I met the woman who would become my wife, and she saved me.*

Andrew had realized a few days ago that even though he wanted to do this whole production himself, go full-on indie, that maybe having another set of eyes on the script, an objective individual, was a good idea.

It was rare that I handled passion projects like this —the people in charge didn't tend to like anyone disagreeing with them—but I liked Andrew and his story, and he seemed like he'd actually listen. My contract said he had to, or I walked, so there was also that.

I checked the map on my phone that I'd been sent of the set. Rather than being on a familiar sound stage in L.A., we were in the middle of Salt Lake City, because that's where most of the movie was being filmed. Somewhere in this giant building, there was supposed to be a room set up for a table read. But none of the doors in this image matched what I saw in front of me.

You lost? A voice from the past whispered in my

ear, and I was instantly back on set for the first time, twenty years ago.

When I'd seen him for the first time, there hadn't been sparks or choirs of singing angels. We were twelve, I barely knew I liked boobs and had no idea I was going to like dicks just as much. All I knew was that he was a friendly face, smiling and not looking mean and impatient like the adults around us.

Yeah, I'd admitted shyly. *I'm supposed to be on the set of Donovan's Wilde Ride.*

He'd grabbed my hand and tugged me in a completely different direction than the one I'd been walking in. *I'm Donovan, I know where you're supposed to be. Actually, I'm Austin.*

Elijah, actually Eli. I'd wanted to sound as cool and casual as he did.

Oh yeah, you're going to be my new best friend. Wicked.

I was pretty sure he'd meant *new best friend* on the show, but we'd become fast friends in real life too.

"Jaws. You lost?" Andrew's voice broke into my traipse into the past. It was my understanding he called very few people by their real names, and I was lucky my nickname wasn't food-related.

I shook away the shadows of memory—where did those come from? "Can't find the room for the table read."

He leaned in to look at my phone over my shoulder. "Right." He grabbed my shoulders and spun me a quarter turn. "I tried to tell them a map without an indicator of north was just a picture."

Sure enough, now that I could tell which way was which, I knew exactly where I needed to be. "Thanks."

"Let's go." Andrew fell into step beside me, and we headed to our destination.

Most of the actors were already here, seated around the table, shuffling through screenplays and chatting with each other. Though I'd worked with several people in the room before, I still got starstruck being surrounded by so many of them.

Just as many of the faces were new this time, though. Andrew wanted to work with some of the actors who had done movies for him when he owned Smut Central. Give them a chance to switch to clothed theater if they were interested.

He put me in the seat next to him at the front of the room, we all introduced ourselves, and dove into our first reading of the screenplay.

Today my biggest job was to listen and make notes. I had thoughts about what kind of changes were needed, but I'd get a more complete picture as I heard the way everything was performed.

When I'd been fired from *Donovan*, years ago, when I realized I'd been blacklisted as an actor, I'd been devastated. Seventeen years old and my career was over, and I was certain it was Austin's fault.

He still had his job, though we'd both been equal

participants in the quiet *losing our virginity to each other* scandal, so it must've been his fault.

The first time I was offered the chance to help fix a script, I fell into it easily. I loved the creativity, and I got to step back into this world that had an energy I thrived on.

For the most part I'd gotten over how things ended with Austin, though sometimes the past still slammed into me, like earlier today.

The story was told chronologically, starting when Andrew was younger, but there were also flashbacks later in life, to those same younger years.

He hadn't budged on that when we talked, but I hoped seeing it today, seeing that it was going to be confusing to do things both ways, would change his mind.

Listening to the younger actors go through his growing up was fine—they were great. His teenage years, especially once he hit South American, flowed smoothly too. I scribbled a lot of notes, but they were mostly about polishing things, not about having to make any huge changes.

And then we moved closer to *now*. Adult Andrew talking to his nephew about figuring out his sexuality when he was younger. About how he'd fallen for his best friend at the time. They'd known each other for so long, the attraction was so strong, but they didn't end up together.

I was back in my past again, watching a montage of growing up on set with Austin. Us getting closer, inseparable. People called us brothers, but I was pretty sure most brothers didn't feel about each other the way I had about him.

His first kiss had been on camera, and awkward. He hated doing that in front of the world. So I'd offered to let him have a second chance at a first kiss, away from the cameras.

And *wow* the sparks.

Once again, I shoved aside the memories, and focused on the story instead. It wasn't easy though. Half the flashbacks triggered more glimpses into my life before.

By the time we wrapped up, the urge to flee itched under my skin. I let the after-read chatter wash over me, gathered my things as quickly as I could while still looking calm, and walked from the room.

I didn't run. I didn't speed walk. I never let anyone see the panic. But I needed air. To get out of here and let a good drive push away these ghosts.

"Jaws, wait up." Andrew caught up to me when I was almost to my car.

I paused, but my fist clenched without my permission. Not because of him, but because I was still here.

"You still feeling the vibe after Day One?" He asked. Excitement shone on his face.

"I am." And I meant it. His was a great story, with a lot of potential. My toes tried to tap inside my shoes, and I curled them to keep them still. My fingers drummed against my leg in response.

Andrew frowned. "Am I keeping you from something?"

"No. I just… Sometimes being back on the set hits me harder than others." I didn't tell anyone the full story about my past, but Andrew knew enough that my reply would make sense.

He nodded. "I get it. Do this—Take I-80 west, out toward the lake. There's zero Hollywood feel, and it'll make you miss the ocean."

"It's a lake. Won't it be just like any other beach?"

Andrew snort-laughed. "Sorry. No. I mean, they call it a beach, but… You'll see."

Whatever. As long as it got me some air. I pointed my rental in the direction he said, and drove. Within about fifteen minutes, I'd left most of the city behind, and about half an hour later, I was driving alongside the lake.

I saw what he meant. It wasn't so much the kind of beach I was used to as a collection of scrub brush and flies. It was quiet, though, and pretty in its own desolate way.

This was where I should stop, maybe take a few pictures, then go back to my hotel. I wasn't ready for that, so I kept driving. The freeway signs said Wendover was one-hundred-ten miles away. I'd been there once. It was a small Nevada town that didn't know it was small.

Maybe I needed that right now.

The solitude helped calm my mind, and lulled me into a sort of driving-trance that let me keep my attention on the road, but didn't require much else from me. I was maybe forty-five minutes into the drive, at least thirty miles from anything in either direction, when my car started to slow down.

"What are you...?" I glanced at the gauges and scowled. I was out of gas.

I managed to coast to the side of the road before the engine stalled completely.

Well, this sucked.

I dialed the rental car company and they promised to send someone out, but it would be at least an hour. Why hadn't I checked the tank before I left? Did the past really have me that distracted? I'd promised myself a long time ago that memories of Austin wouldn't get under my skin, and now...

A car pulled onto the shoulder ahead of me, the taillights turned white, and they backed up toward me. Cool. A random savior. I'd probably had enough solitude for the day.

I slipped on a smile, and approached the new car.

And then the driver climbed out.

My entire past tumbled in on me at once. Everything I'd been trying to escape since the table read. Those threads of heartache and betrayal I wished didn't still have this hold on me.

The man approaching me had a lot more tattoos than when I'd known him. He was definitely older and held himself with more confidence. But the little boy I'd known still shone in his eyes.

His smile was the most disconcerting thing about

him, though. It was broad and genuine. Like he was actually happy to see me. Like he hadn't destroyed my entire career because I was stupid enough to fall in love with him when we were both teenagers. "Elijah?"

Austin. Did I conjure him from thin air with my haunted memories?

It didn't matter. It was tempting to walk to Nevada rather than talk to him.

4
joystick

THERE WAS a hell of a lot of nothing between California and Utah, and it was called Nevada. But I'd known that when I chose to make the drive, rather than fly.

I needed the perfect place for my first restaurant, which I'd planned as much as I could without acting after a couple of months in Italy with my new friends, Raul and Diego, and learning from them. I was pretty sure I'd either put it in L.A. or Salt Lake, because both had their own reasons for being the perfect place for the gimmick, but I had to check the places in between, too. Just in case.

Also, I was in the mood to drive. When I was younger, I had a plan. My best friend—the first boy I fell in love with—and I were going to drive across the country. As soon as the studio admitted we were old enough to go off on our own without becoming a publicity nightmare, we'd planned to take the first of many road trips to see the world on our own terms, not on a tour docket for the TV show.

I still liked the impromptu road trips, and most of the time I convinced myself I didn't miss Eli when I took them.

This one had an additional goal, though. I was hoping once I reached my destination, I'd run into Kandace again. Possibly on purpose. I'd never had a one night stand I couldn't get out of my head, and she's earned that spot. The entire trip to Italy, regardless of the fucked-up way it started, had been a blast. Once in a lifetime kind of experience, because of the way it all unfolded, but Kandace...

She was brilliant and shy and bold and smart and incredible. Sure it had only been one night, but I was hooked and wanted to know more.

There wasn't much traffic on this stretch of road, and I was miles from anything in either direction, when I noticed a car on the other side of the freeway pull over.

Sucky place to break down. It'd be easy to ignore them. Keep driving. They probably had a phone, everyone did, and it may be something as simple as a flat tire.

You're selfish. Self-absorbed. Why did you think they fired me?

That voice was from so many years ago, but it barked in my mind every time I thought about passing someone who looked like they needed help.

God damn it.

There was a police turn around a little further down the road, and yeah, I wasn't supposed to use it, but who would care? I flipped a U-turn and headed back to the car that had pulled over. If they didn't need help, I'd be on my way, and if they did, it would be a good thing I stopped. It wasn't as though I was on a schedule.

I pulled over several yards away and backed up to get closer. As I got out of my car and approached theirs, they stepped out to greet me.

My breath caught and my brain stalled. Holy shit. "Elijah?" It had been more than a decade, but I knew those eyes. The messy dark hair and the penetrating gaze. The scowl.

"Austin." His voice was flat.

It had been years since anyone but bankers and my mother called me that. "Hi. And it's Joystick now."

"I'm not calling you that. Why would you call yourself that?"

A far better response than him spitting in my face. "I don't want people remembering Donovan." The TV show we'd grown up on together. The series that made me a household name and destroyed me for any future chance of being myself if I clung to the character.

"That makes two of us." Eli's voice was flat.

Speaking of... "Flat tire?" I nodded at his car. My mind was starting to catch up. To figure out I was talking to *him*. He'd refused my calls for years, and I finally gave up. He blamed me, and I understood why, though it wasn't my fault.

When he and I gave our virginity to each other, word had gotten out. Of course, because nothing was quiet in Hollywood. But the showrunners were determined that their shining star, the teenager millions of boys wanted to be and just as many girls wanted to fuck—me—wouldn't hit public gossip pages as some sort of queer boy.

They told me Eli left. They told him he was a danger to my career and fired him. I never considered the possibility I'd been lied to until I ran into him a few years later and he let me have an earful.

"Out of gas," Eli said.

A lot of things had felt like fate over the last few months. Random, awkward things I couldn't possibly have planned on my own. This had to be one of them. Finally, a chance to talk to him again. To actually apologize. There's no way he was holding a grudge still, fifteen years later. "I'll give you a lift to the closest town, to grab some."

He didn't answer. We were in the middle of nowhere, his car was on empty, and he was fucking hesitating.

I hated that we'd become this. I looked at him and I couldn't help but see my former best friend. My first lover.

Eli's nostrils flared, and he nodded. "Sure. A lift would be nice."

I motioned to the car. "Hop on in."

"You finally got the El Camino," he said as I slid into the driver's seat.

"I did. I love it. I'm glad you get to see it."

"Hmm."

Maybe stopping was a mistake, but this still felt like the universe was trying to tell me something. He was the reason I'd considered pulling over, he was the one who needed help. "You here for work? You live here?" Can I buy you dinner some night this week? You'll like Kandace. She's responsible like you.

"Hmm."

This was going well. "What are you doing these days?" I'd heard rumors, but no details. Anyone who was close with Eli was aware he didn't want anything to do with me.

"Bit of this, bit of that."

A longer answer with no more information. "That's specific," I teased. Anything to lighten the atmosphere in here.

"Look, I appreciate the ride." Eli's tone made it sound like he wasn't certain he meant it. "And I think fate's a cruel bitch that it was you who stopped for me. You, of all people, in the middle of fucking nowhere. But you don't owe me conversation or anything. You explained yourself the last time we talked."

I did. And my explanation was *I'm sorry, I had no idea. I never would've let it happen.* "Does that mean the past is behind us? I have a whole new name. We could start over."

"We really can't."

The only time either of us spoke on the rest of the ride to Wendover was when he called the rental company to tell them not to bother meeting him at his car.

Fucking. Awkward.

"Let me buy you lunch," I said as we pulled into the gas station. "We can catch up. Shoot the shit. Whatever."

"I'm good, thanks. You should stay here though. Eat, or whatever, and I'll grab a cab back."

"I don't think many cabs, Ubers, whatever, run out of this place."

Eli shrugged. "I'll figure it out."

"At least let me pay for the gas," I offered as we stepped into the small building. A rack of keychains stood near the register, and I couldn't help my smile. Some were novelty phrases, and some were license plates, both Utah and Nevada.

That had been part of our road trip plan too—keychain at every stop, to commemorate our trips. One of them had an *E* on it, and I added it to the bill as I paid for gas and a canister for it.

Eli raised an eyebrow when I handed it all over, gave a quick shake of his head, and shoved the keychain into his jeans pocket. That was something, wasn't it?

"So, I'm heading to the casino across the street." I nodded in that direction. "If you want to join me for lunch, I'll be there for at least an hour."

Allyson Lindt

"I won't."

Sigh. "It was good seeing you again."

Eli shook his head. "Hmm."

I waited in the casino's diner, the way I said I would, but Eli didn't show up. I wasn't surprised, but it did hurt. When it came time to pay the bill, I fished my wallet out of my pocket.

Something fell to the ground.

I crouched to find a keychain resting against my foot, and a smile threatened as I picked it up.

Glad you're not here.

Oh.

Eli was long gone when I got outside, of course. And his car was gone too, when I reached that part of the freeway.

That sucked.

This was where I should let it go. He'd made his thoughts clear. We hadn't been friends since we were kids.

But seeing him again today... It was meant to be.

I rarely used my connections in Hollywood, but for this I was willing to make a call. I dialed my agent. "I want to know where Elijah is. What he's doing."

"You don't already know?" Randy sounded shocked.

"I wouldn't be asking if I did."

As Randy explained to me that Eli was a fixer, an odd feeling blossomed inside.

"I want to know what movie he's working on in Utah," I said. "Please."

34

Because yeah, I was going to make things right with Eli.

5
kandace

IT'D BEEN five months since I was in Milan.

Every time I talked to Carly, or caught the scent of good espresso, or saw a Donovan meme on my son's social media, I had tiny flashbacks to that night with Joystick.

Was that normal?

For instance, right now I was standing on a makeshift sound stage, people rushing around me, cameras on one side of the room.... I should be completely focused on finding Andrew, and instead I was wondering if Joystick ever missed this.

It was bedlam here. The kind of chaos that Andrew was probably thriving on. The kind of setting that made me want to start writing up lists and schedules and spreadsheets.

I'd liked that wild side of me, with Joystick. With the sexy stranger in a foreign land. I'd liked letting loose for the night.

"*Coming through.*" A shout startled me, and I pressed my back to the wall to let a pair of men carrying a large wooden trunk pass by.

I also liked the order that was my normal life. That when I had Lucas home for Christmas break, I had a chance to mother my fastidious boy and pretend he wasn't an adult in his first year of college now. We shopped. Bought him new clothes, a few more pieces of furniture for his apartment.

And I spent an unreasonable amount of those trips grateful that he'd grown out of that phase where he wanted all the Donovan merchandise. It was already weird that there were pictures hanging on Lucas's wall of the teenage version of the adult man who gave me the best sex of my life. That Lucas loved those shows in syndication, that a lot of kids his age did, *because of the super obvious gay vibes, Mom.*

"Excuse me." I tried to flag down people as they hurried past. A couple of them glanced in my direction, and one or two said, "I'll be right with you," but no one stopped.

Andrew tried to invite me down here while they were still doing the initial construction, but December was a busy month at The Raphael Group, with everyone pushing for last minute money or sales or spending or something.

I should've made time before the place was packed. And why was this map so crappy? Where was Andrew's temporary office?

I was drawing in a deep breath to shout and draw

attention, when a man stopped in front of me. He was about Andrew's age, maybe a little younger. At least ten years my junior.

About Joystick's age.

Enough, me. It had been an incredible night, and I wouldn't deny that, but I was putting anything but the memories out of my head. If I lived in Mental Milan forever, I'd never get anything done. Ever again.

"Can I help you find something?" He was sexy in a smart, responsible kind of way.

The kind of guy I'd probably be much happier fucking long term.

It was time to knock it off. Seriously. I'd never been that *I'd jump his bones* with every single guy I met. I needed balance. I could probably still have some fun, but not *sleep with a stranger in Italy* kinds of wild. "I'm looking for Andrew Newton," I said.

He dragged his gaze over me, and I swore he lingered on my hips and breasts before finally looking me in the eye. The staring wasn't enough for me to call him out on it, especially with the heat he sent spilling through me.

Did he look familiar? Was he one of Andrew's actors?

No. Because I didn't watch Andrew's old work. *Any* of it, because that was creepy.

"Are you an actress?" Smart Stranger asked. "One of his previous acquaintances?"

Did he just make the same assumption I had? He

thought I used to be... in porn? Me? My laugh slipped out. "No. *God* that would be awkward. I'm his sister."

He furrowed his brow and tilted his head, studying me again. "His sister is older. A lot older."

"Ten years is a lot when you're twenty. Not when you're in your forties."

"No. I didn't mean..." He sighed. "You don't look it."

I should be flattered he thought I was younger, but I was hung up on the implication that I was old. "Do you want to see my ID? They checked it before they let me onto the lot. Who are you?"

He rubbed the back of his neck. "The asshole who got off on the wrong foot with Kandace Newton."

"Kind of a long name." I was going to lean toward *flattered*, because he really was cute, and he was trying. "Should I call you *Asshole*? I'm not sure I'm comfortable with that."

He extended his hand with a light *heh*. "I'm Eli. The fixer."

"I'd make a joke about it being nice to meet someone else who cleans up my brother's messes, but I'm not an asshole." Did I really say that? Who was I? I would never say something like that. "I'm sorry, I didn't mean..." Crap. I shook his hand.

"Am I ever going to live that down?"

I smiled. "I don't hold grudges, life is too short."

"Let me make it up to you anyway," he said. "I'll buy you dinner tonight, and spend the hours between now and then thinking up smoother ways to tell you you're beautiful. We'll have an actual conversation, and get to know each other."

Ah. The way he slid into that line, the awkwardness must be an act. His charm came off as sincere, but I suddenly doubted it really was. "No. If you could point me to Andrew, that would be fantastic."

"This way." A frown flickered across Eli's face, and vanished again, snatched away in the chaos.

I hated thinking this way, having to question motives, examine every move and action and intention, but it came with my line of work. I was a partner in an angel investor firm that focused mainly on tech companies. When I joined them a few years back, I wanted to give everyone an equal chance. Take all the words at face value, rely strictly on the data presented to me and the words that were used.

After all, some people weren't great at presenting, but had brilliant ideas. I quickly learned that the opposite was just as true. The pretty words, the data that looked good on paper, the stories spun to get access to our money, were frequently just smoke and mirrors.

Once I started seeing the illusion in one place, I couldn't help but see it everywhere. Eli was giving off a conflicting series of vibes, and it was always safer to err on the side of caution.

That didn't stop me from watching him, appreciating the view, as he led me across the warehouse floor. I could look but not touch. I could also still wonder why he seemed so familiar.

Was it because I was hoping to run into someone famous on set?

And he was gorgeous. Would it have hurt that much to take him up on his offer for dinner?

It would if he kept using lines like *spend hours thinking of ways to tell you you're beautiful.* That was straight out of a back screenplay. One or more of his, possibly. Or one of those high-heat romance novels Carly loved.

"In here." Eli gestured toward an open office door on the opposite end of the building from where I'd been looking.

Andrew was sitting at a desk, his laptop in front of him, a cup of coffee to his left, and nothing else in here. Standard operating procedure for Andrew— things were temporary. Simplicity was key.

He looked up and grinned. "Candy Cane. You've met Jaws."

I'd ask where the nickname came from, but Andrew never had a reason. He liked alliteration and he typically disliked real names. "I did."

"You good?" Eli's question was clipped. The smooth-talking smarty had vanished.

Not really surprised, though I wanted to be. I'd hoped he was genuine. "Yes. Thank you."

With that, Eli walked out and closed the door behind himself.

"*I did*?" Andrew's voice was hard to read. "That's it?"

What was he looking for from me? "Did you want a dissertation on every staff member I meet?"

"Nah." Andrew shrugged. "I just figured Jaws was the kind of person you'd hit it off with."

"Because…?"

"He's responsible. Like you." Andrew winked.

Uh-huh. I shook my head in amused disbelief. When Andrew was a kid, it was true. Hell, when he was eighteen, he was backpacking across South America when an ex-girlfriend of his dropped their baby on my porch.

Biologically, Andrew was Lucas's father. In every other way, he was Uncle Andrew, and I was *Mom*. I'd raised Lucas. He was my son.

Andrew had also grown up a lot since then, with a big spurt of maturity when he met his wife, Susan, and as much as he liked to still pretend he was irresponsible and reckless, he'd gotten to where he was on his own. "No, he's an asshole, like you." The words came out teasing, in my head they were playful, but I still felt bad saying them out loud. It had taken me years to get comfortable with calling my own brother names like that, and only because he'd coaxed it out of me.

Did I really just say that about someone who worked for him? Regardless of what I thought of Eli, that was inappropriate.

Andrew didn't look fazed. Of course. "I promise

you, he's a very different kind of asshole from me. What did he do?"

"Told me I was pretty and asked me out." That sounded weak. But I had my reasons.

Andrew's feigned shock said he didn't see what those were. "Oh. My. God. He wanted to spend more time with you? He complimented you? Fucking jerk. Do you want me to fire him? I bet he thought the two of you would go somewhere and eat. Talk. About how responsible you both are. That's it, he's out of here. No one buys my sister dinner and gets away with it."

"Knock it off." I didn't appreciate him being the voice of my doubt.

"Consider it knocked. Do you want the grand tour?"

"Can we stop talking about assholes?"

The way Andrew screwed up his face in thought told me I was about to regret the way I phrased my question. "Fortunately for you, we're not filming the anal for another two weeks."

"There's no... Not in a movie like this." Heat flooded my face. Yup, I still got embarrassed about the way he talked about sex, about making porn, the way I talked about ROI and ACOS.

"It's an indie film. Thought I'd try to slip something like that in." He chuckled. "Damn it, I can't believe I just wasted a good anal joke on you. Where's Eli? I want him to write that into the screenplay."

If I let Andrew keep going, he'd never stop. If I

asked him to stop again, that would be worse. "A tour would be great."

Andrew led me through the warehouse, and pointed out various things. The buffet table. The camera crew. The handful of actors. The couple of sound stages that looked eerily like rooms from our house growing up. He'd recreated those a little too well for my suppressed trauma.

I caught glimpses of Eli every so often, and told myself not to stare. To put him out of my mind. Not every puzzle needed to be solved, including and especially his sincerity.

We walked at the edge of a room that looked disturbingly like every classroom in the private high school Andrew and I had attended. Was one of those desks inscribed with the name of the boy I was certain I loved back then? How real was this set?

A large crack sounded behind me, at the same time someone shouted, "Look out."

Before I could spin, a horrific scream of agony filled the room.

6
elijah

FUCK THIS HURT. Probably not as badly as my initial shout implied—that was as much surprise as pain—but the pain in my thumb still throbbed. When I saw the stage light falling toward Kandace and Andrew, I didn't so much think as act.

What did I hope to accomplish? I hadn't thought that far.

"Someone get some ice." Andrew's barked order carried through the room.

Kandace had my wrist and was examining the injury.

"Huh. He got you to hold his hand after all. Tricky bastard," Andrew teased.

Right now? Really?

Kandace shot him a raised eyebrow look, then turned back to me. "It wasn't at that angle before, was it?"

I hadn't really looked, but now I examined my

thumb. "No. It doesn't usually sit at an angle. Are you a doctor?" Stupid question. The screenplay would say that if she was a doctor. Though, come to think of it, the story kind of glossed over her profession.

"No. I'm a mother." Her tone was cool, but in a *let's handle the crisis* kind of way, rather than the icy brush off she gave me earlier.

"I'm so sorry." One of the interns handed over a plastic bag filled with ice. "I tripped. I didn't mean... I'm so sorry."

Everyone was watching us. Me. I didn't care for this kind of attention anyway, but I really didn't want it while I was sitting here trying to bite back the pain.

"Don't they have work to do?" Kandace glanced at Andrew.

Yup, this was the woman from the script. Practical. Decisive. Possibly the smartest person in the room.

Andrew gave a curt nod and whistled sharply. "No one died and no one is going to die. Go do something else."

"Hold this here, in whatever way hurts the least." Kandace pressed the ice pack to my hand.

It was probably the pain talking, but I swore little sparkles danced around her. The actress playing adult-Kandace in the movie didn't hold a candle to her anyway, but I was pretty sure sparkles floated around her now.

Nope, that was the pain making me loopy.

"Should we call an ambulance?" Andrew asked.

Probably a good idea.

Kandace shook her head. "Out here? It'll take too long. I'll drive him."

"If you didn't want the grand tour, you could've just said so," Andrew said.

Kandace glared at him. "Tour's over. You're going to bring that up now?"

They were going to argue now? With my thumb bent like a banana?

"I make jokes in stressful situations. That's what I do." Andrew shrugged.

"Pretty sure the second half of that sentence wasn't necessary." Kandace turned to me. "I'll drive you, if you're okay with that."

Right. I could actually participate in this conversation. "Please."

Andrew stopped Kandace as she and I were walking away. His voice was quiet—who knew that was possible?—but I caught something about her using the company card if there was a bill, and making sure all the workman's comp got filled out.

Kandace joined me again and we walked in silence to the parking lot. Which wasn't great. Without the bedlam to observe, my brain was free to home in on *fuck, this hurts*. I wasn't sure I trusted myself to speak, though. What came out would either be whimper, or something else that might bring that stony mask back she'd put on earlier.

I hadn't meant to offend her. I never did things like ask strangers out to lunch, especially with lines about them being pretty. Joystick probably wouldn't have fucked things up so badly.

Great—he was the last person I needed to be thinking about.

Ooh, I could play the *which car does she drive* game. Something practical. Subtle, but classy. Something that wouldn't stand out, but was pristine.

The lights blinked and the alarm chirped on a candy red Mercedes SUV, and she pointed us in that direction.

As we climbed into the truck, my thumb throbbed with insistence. So much for blocking that out.

"It's a little bit of a drive, but I'll try to hurry." Kandace sounded sympathetic.

"I'll be okay until then." I managed to make the words sound convincing, but I couldn't hide my grunt when I tried to put my seatbelt on, and another jolt of pain spiked up my arm.

The way Kandace furrowed her brow looked concerned rather than annoyed. "I'll help." She leaned across me from her seat, to grab the belt.

She smelled like lilacs and fresh soap, and I wasn't sure which was worse—that I wanted to lean in and sniff her hair, or that I was half hard from her fingers brushing my skin.

When she snapped the belt in place and straightened in her seat, her face was flushed pink.

The silence that settled back in was awkward. How was I supposed to clear up the earlier misunderstanding? I might be wittier if I had all night to come up with my half of the script... and could think more clearly.

"*Oh.*" The startled noise Kandace made had me concerned. "I know why I recognize you."

No. Please no. Please let her be mistaken.

"You're from Donovan's Wilde Ride. You were his best friend."

Fuck. "I'd rather not do this." There was no reason to take my issues with my past out on her, but my politeness tended to vanish when people wanted to gush about the show or Austin.

"Do... what?" Kandace asked.

"Any number of things that are about to happen. I'd rather not talk about the show. If you loved it, if you hated it, I'm grateful-slash-sorry you had that experience. I can't introduce you or your son to Austin, and we're not secret lovers who have kept our life together hidden from the media for the last fifteen years."

That should about cover it.

Kandace glanced at me, her expression... sympathetic? "Okay."

"Like that?" The conversation never went this way.

She shrugged. "You don't want to talk about it, and now that I know why you're familiar, I can stop wondering."

"And now I'm the jerk again." I couldn't get this right.

One corner of her mouth tugged up. "Believe it or

not, I get it. The way people react when they find out who my brother is… I get it."

I'd had people tell me that in the past—that they understood why I didn't like talking about the show or my co-start—but that was typically followed by another question or statement about the same topic.

With Kandace, I believed she meant it. That she understood and that she'd drop the subject.

"Okay." A chuckle slipped out when I realized I'd just parroted her.

Her laugh was light. Addictive. "You do have me at a disadvantage, though."

"How do you figure?"

"I've read the screenplay you're working on—you know a lot more about me than I do about you."

There was that. "Are you going to try to tell me none of that is exaggerated?" I'd heard Andrew spin making an egg into an epic odyssey of trial and tribulation, and there were parts of his script that were extra-extra.

"The parts about me are pretty accurate." Kandace navigated traffic without pause, as if this was a route she drove on a regular basis, and it was no big deal. "There are parts that are close to accurate. I did, in fact, tend to Mrs. Havisham, though I didn't know what to make of her in her wedding dress, with her desiccated cake, the first time I made her acquaintance."

The elements of her story whirred in my brain and

clicked together in a whole picture that was not one of her. "That's Great Expectations."

"Is it?" A hint of playfulness slid into her voice.

I wanted to say *you're prettier than Gwyneth Paltrow, and so far a lot kinder too,* but the compliment referencing the wrong character plus a movie adaptation might strike me out. "Almost certain of it."

"Oh. I thought it was Andrew's movie." Kandace didn't sound for a second like she'd thought that. "Well, then the part about helping an entire Soviet submarine crew defect? That's all true."

I raised an eyebrow. "That's *The Hunt for Red October*, and you definitely don't look like Sean Connery."

"No?" We stopped at a light, and she made a flicking motion with her arm that might have been writing or wielding a sword. "Bond. James Bond."

"Your accent needs a little work." And this was fun. "Are you sure you've read the script?"

"Do I need to? I lived it, after all." She still sounded light.

This wasn't what I'd expected at all. Did that mean I had expectations? Well, yeah. I'd built up an entire reality about the people I'd met on paper. "I'm actually thinking the story doesn't do you justice at all."

"I'm boring in the movie, aren't I?" Some of her cheer vanished.

I didn't hesitate with my answer. "Definitely not."

"It's okay. I'm boring in real life too." Now the fun was definitely gone.

"You're not that either. You're the most fascinating person I've talked to since I arrived." I meant it.

Her tight smile said she didn't believe me, and she turned into a clinic parking lot. "It's okay. I'm not saying it's a bad thing. I know who I am. I'll wait here for you and take you back to your hotel when you're done."

And now she'd shut the topic of her down. What was I doing wrong?

"You don't have to wait. Don't get me wrong, I'd love to keep talking, and since we're not having dinner…" I needed to drop that. "If you're gone when I get out, I'll understand."

"I'm your ride. I'll wait."

Inside, they showed me to a room within a few minutes. The nurse took my vitals, poked at my hand enough to make me want to scream, and said someone would be with me soon.

I spent the next couple of hours alone with my thoughts. Of Austin. Of Kandace. Of how muddled this entire trip was making my head.

I'd scrolled through all my social media feeds multiple times, checked my email relentlessly, and lost more match-three games than I could count by the time a doctor saw me. Good thing my right thumb still worked. They shuffled me through X-ray, put a splint on my thumb, and sent me on my way with a list of instructions.

It had been nearly three hours, and I was surprised to wander into the parking lot and see Kandace's SUV was still here. It didn't look like she was in it, though.

Her voice drifted from behind me, half a conversation. Like that, my frustration vanished, and a smile tugged at my mouth. Because I got to see her, a woman I barely knew. Was that weird?

I turned to see her walking toward me, phone to her ear. When she met my gaze, she held up a finger, which I assumed meant *just a minute*.

"Sorry. Work stuff," she said as she joined me.

"I hope I wasn't keeping you from important things." From what I knew, when Andrew sold Smut Central a few years ago, he'd essentially put Kandace in charge of the estate. She'd re-invested his money into tech, and was now a partner in an angel investor firm.

She knew more about numbers and funds than I could ever hope to learn.

And she was shaking her head. "No. I can do most of my work via phone. Not a big deal."

"Anything interesting?" I was genuinely curious. "Like, a big... I don't know... technical thing that's coming that I should be excited about? Or do you have to keep that top secret, like lawyers."

"Not like lawyers, more like people worried about patent issues." Her frown was back, and then gone again in an instant. "Unless you mean my *other* job. The top secret one where I don't tell anyone I'm a

Hollywood madame. Oops." She covered her mouth with her fingertips, as if she'd let a big secret slip.

What was she…? Pieces were moving in my head, but not clicking together to form a picture.

"I'll take you back to where you're staying," she said.

There wasn't a lot of talking as she drove, but my mind was still working. Clicking. Stopping. Whirring to life again…

She seemed to be working really hard to convince me she was someone else…

Oh.

Maybe I wasn't the only one trying to leave a good impression.

She pulled up in front of the place that had been converted into a boarding home for not-local members of the crew to stay in. When she stopped the car, I was tempted to invite her up to my room. To talk. For something else.

A woman like this deserved more than a one-night stand, but I wasn't ready to give up her company yet.

I shifted in my seat, so I was facing her, and she turned to me, curiosity on her face.

"You keep trying to convince me you lead a secret, fascinating life," I said. "But you're already intriguing to me as you are."

Kandace's laugh was abrupt. "I'm a soccer mom, but my kid doesn't play soccer. I'm schedules and order and plans that span into the next decade without a lot of wiggle room. I'm not the woman men call pretty *just because* and mean it." She puffed out her cheeks in a long sigh. "And I don't know why I just told you all of that, but I am who I am."

I placed a finger under her chin and raised her head so I could meet her gaze. "I really did mean it, even if it came off like a line. I was sincere." She was stunning, and her personality was so real. So the opposite of everything I hated about Hollywood. Even now, staring into her eyes, I was drawn in. Captivated.

Before I fully registered what I was doing, I tilted my head, leaned in, and brushed my lips over hers.

She was going to pull away and slap me.

But she didn't. She leaned into me with soft lips and a softer gasp.

And the sparks. *Holy fuck.* I needed more. I slid my hand to the back of her neck, to grip tightly, and deepened the kiss. She tasted like breath mints and coffee, and *God*, I couldn't get enough. When she clenched my shirt in her fists, when she whimpered against my mouth, I was instantly hard.

I wanted to pull her into my lap and explore her with kisses, but I didn't want to break away. Didn't want to shatter this moment.

Kandace leaned harder into me, and I felt her lose her balance. But she caught herself without ending the lip-lock. Her hand landed on my thigh, brushing my cock through my jeans, and I couldn't help my groan.

She giggled into the kiss, and danced her fingers along the outline of my erection.

Fuck, fuck, fuck, fuck, fuck. As in, I wanted to fuck her right here in the parking lot. I glided my good hand along the curve of her neck, over her breast, to tease a nipple through her clothing.

She gasped and pressed into my touch.

We were making out in a hotel back lot like horny teenagers, electricity wrapping around us, and I wanted—needed—to keep going.

A rap on the window sent my heart plummeting into my feet, and we both jumped. I turned to see a police officer standing next to the vehicle.

Oops.

The window slid down between us. That must've been Kandace, because my brain was still in my dick.

"I'm going to have to ask you two to take this inside. Or somewhere else. One of the residents across the street complained." The officer looked like he wanted to be anywhere but here.

I couldn't help my laugh. "Yeah. Sorry about that. We're going."

"Thanks." He turned away quickly.

I turned back to Kandace to find her laughing with her face in her hands. "That was incredible," I said. "You're incredible. *Now* can I buy you lunch tomorrow?"

"Okay." Her reply was muffled.

I grasped her wrist to pull her hand away and

look her in the eye. "Enjoy the rest of your day, Kandace Newton."

"You too."

I'd kiss her again, but I doubted it would be any easier to stop the second time, so I forced myself to exit the vehicle.

A goofy giddiness filled me as I headed up to my room. I wasn't a hermit or celibate or anything so drastic. I dated whoever caught my eye, but I rarely clicked with anyone.

Kandace though… And then we were making out in her car. How…?

Incredible.

Those lips. Her eyes. That brain…

I let myself into my room. If I wasn't careful, I'd spend all night thinking about that one moment. Fun, but not productive. I checked my mail, and frowned at the message from my agent that simply said *you need to see this.*

I clicked the link, and waited impatiently for the page to load.

Former Child Star Donovan Breaking into Food?

The article was about Austin. Who was apparently thinking of opening a restaurant. Here. And the pictures they'd chosen were one current, and one of him and me, from the TV show. Standing next to each other. Grinning like idiots.

Because I had been an idiot back then.

Like that, my mood wilted. Why was he back in my life again? Everywhere. Suddenly?

7
kandace

It had been more than a day, and I swore I still felt Eli's lips on mine. Making out in the car—did adults really do that? Not that I had a clue, since I hadn't even been the kid who did that.

Then again, when I thought about Joystick, I still felt some pretty intense tingles much lower on my body. But Joystick was months ago, and Eli was here. Now.

Which was why I was going through my closet, looking at and discarding everything I owned as looking too old. Too stuffy. Too professional. Why didn't I own a single outfit that said casual, like I didn't try too hard, but I know I still look incredible?

Because the entire contents of my wardrobe were on my bed now, it was time to do another pass.

My phone rang, and Lucas's name and face popped on the screen. A distraction. Thank God. I put the phone on speaker and left it on my dresser. "Hey, hon. What's up?"

"I. Am. Freaking out." The panic in his voice was more along the lines of this-is-about-a-cute-boy panic, and not someone-just-stole-my-laptop panic.

I picked up a T-shirt with lacy shoulders and a flower print on the front that screamed old-lady-who-wishes-she-was-young. Which, I did if I was dating men more than 10 years my junior. I tossed it into a new pile. "What's going on?"

"You know the guy I was telling you about?"

"Broad shoulders, square jaw, giant brain?"

Lucas sighed. "Yes. He's coming over to study social sciences with me tonight, and I need to make snacks. They have to say this is incredible, I can't get it anywhere else, without looking like I tried too hard."

Yup, this was my kid. "Do you have time to shop? If not, what's in the house?" Helping him to figure out what to make was far better than thinking about my wardrobe.

"I only have three hours. Maybe I can have something delivered if I need. I have the basics in the house."

Which meant something different for him than for most college students. He was an internet-taught-chef, and his version of whipping something up tended to involve at least an hour of prep, and many raw ingredients.

"What about those tarts," I asked. "Those are fast. Good."

The way Lucas huffed, that was a big miss on my part. "Tarts, for a study not-date? Are you even trying?"

What was I thinking? I held up and discarded two more tops. "Do you have sausage in the house?"

"Not until he gets here." Lucas snorted. "But seriously, no. I have prosciutto. Pepperoni."

Prosciutto sounded a bit fancy for someone who didn't want to serve tarts. "What about those mini calzones you made over Christmas break. Those were fast and incredible."

Another huff. "That's a brand-new recipe. I can't serve that to a stranger."

"You'll never be happy with it, you know that." Perfection. Another thing we had in common. "But unless he's a food critic for Zagat's—"

"Don't even joke, Mom."

I smiled while I rolled my eyes, and discarded a pair of high-waisted jeans that screamed mom jeans. "He's going to love it, and then next time, what you make will be even better. The only place you'll have to go is up."

It was a horrible thing to say, and I didn't feel that way about his cooking. But I knew he did, and this would be hope to him.

"Okay." He didn't sound convinced. "But only because I only have two hours and forty-five minutes now. What are you doing, by the way?"

Heat rushed into my cheeks. "Getting ready for a date. But I don't know what to wear." Something I hadn't done a lot of while he was growing up, but I hadn't done a lot of it before he arrived, either.

He was forever encouraging me to find a guy. To get laid. His uncle's influence, I assumed.

"Anyone I know?" Lucas asked.

"Unlikely." I hated lying to him. I hadn't even told him Santa was real when he was a kid. The only way I justified the decision now was because he didn't know Eli, Lucas simply worshiped a character Eli had played on TV years ago.

Which was the number one reason I wasn't mentioning names now.

"What about the shirt with the lace sleeves and the flower graphic?" Lucas asked.

"The one that screams grandma?"

He gave a short laugh. "Nothing about you screams grandma, Mom. Wear that with the jeans that have the tears in the thighs—the pair you refuse to throw out—leggings underneath and pull your hair up."

"Okay, so I'll look like an eighties music video reject instead." Should I wear my slouch socks and pink Reeboks, too?

"You'll be comfortable, and he's not going to be looking at your outfit, he's going to be imagining what's underneath it."

Yup, definitely Andrew's influence in there. But I was out of time. "Fine. Thank you. Have fun tonight."

"You too. Love you, Mom." Lucas hung up.

The drive to the lot where they were filming was torture. More than an hour in the car to second-guess all of my life choices that lead up to this point, especially the jeans that were definitely comfy, but were also worn this way because my thighs rubbed together when I walked, and now I was advertising that fact.

But I didn't have time to turn around and go back, and the longer I drove, the more that became the case.

When I got to the lot, it was a lot easier for me to find the crew this time. There was a flow to the place that was like organized chaos, and once I put my trepidation of a new place aside, I felt exactly how things were supposed to flow.

Within a few moments, I'd found the camera crew and actors. But Eli was nowhere to be seen.

Andrew was here though, watching filming from the background. "Rumor is, you're going out with my fixer."

"Rumor is right. Is that a problem?"

Andrew studied me. "You look like you know he doesn't care what you're wearing."

Hurt splintered inside me, and I smothered it with anger blended with apathy. "Since when are you a fashionista?"

"I'm male. You're hinting at as much skin as you're hiding."

In the background, the director yelled *cut* for the fifth time in as many minutes.

It wasn't like I'd tossed on a teddy and thrown a trench coat over it. Also, I didn't like that kind of analysis from him. "Gross."

"I'm being objective, not creepy. And I'm not trying to be mean."

One of the problems with Andrew was, when he let the teasing fall away, he got blunt. Okay, that usually wasn't a problem, but today I didn't appreciate it.

The director yelled *cut* again, and the round of groans that rose up was notable.

"Are you done?" I asked Andrew.

"Overall? Unlikely. For now… I'm fine with it, you look fine, as long as you don't make him quit." Andrew held up a finger and screwed up his face in thought. "Scratch that. As long as he doesn't give me a reason to fire him. Fully serious this time. Make him deserve you."

I was pretty sure there was concern and a compliment hidden in there.

"He's over here, by the way." Andrew nodded to the side of the set, and led me toward Eli, who was sitting in a folding chair and hunched over a laptop.

"Cut," the director yelled again.

Eli pushed his glasses onto his forehead and rubbed his eyes. He radiated stress, but he was still sexy.

His gaze landed on me, and his smile pushed away the scowl lines around his eyes and on his forehead. "Kandace. Hey."

Talking about making a girl feel warm and fuzzy. "Hey."

"Yeah, I'm done here." It was possible Andrew sounded annoyed, but I wasn't paying attention.

"Cut." The director's scream shattered any dream-like, unrealistic dome that might be forming around Eli and me. "This is not working."

Andrew looked at Eli, who was already setting his laptop aside.

"I'll be right back," Eli said to me, and the two of them crossed to the director.

The shouting had stopped, and the animated-but-quiet arguing had started between Andrew and the director. I might not be familiar with this specific industry, but I knew what kind of things happened when creative egos had differences of opinions, and I didn't need to hear what they were saying to know that was what was happening here.

Eli was the only one who looked calm, but his mood seemed contagious.

My phone rang, and I grabbed it and answered without looking at the screen. "Yeah."

"Oh, my God, Kandace. I'm so sorry to call you on a Saturday." Lindsay sounded panicked in a far more serious way than Lucas had earlier. She was the firm's social media manager and tended to keep odd hours because of it.

I also know she wouldn't call if it wasn't critical. "It's okay. What's up?"

"The company that's part of your incubator had a

data breach. Someone is in all of their social media accounts, which gives them access to anything shared with us, which means they're spamming the fuck out of some of our feeds and draining your corporate card on ads."

That was cluster-fucky on a whole new scale. "You're on the social media side of things?"

"Yes."

"I'll take care of the rest." Except I didn't have a computer. How much of this could I do from my phone? A lot, but not all.

I needed to start somewhere. I was in the middle of calls and mental calculations when Eli returned. I wasn't sure where Andrew had gone and right now I didn't care.

"Everything all right?" Eli asked.

"I need a laptop. A desk. Where's Andrew?" Work-mode Kandace was very different from hadn't-dated-much Kandace, and right now she needed things done.

Eli shook his head. "Making phone calls. Something. He didn't file an itinerary with me." As he talked, he clicked through his computer, closed it up, and handed it to me, along with a keycard. "Use my office."

I hadn't meant to kick him out of his workspace. I watched him, puzzled, as he patted down his pockets, and produced a pen.

"Hand," he said.

I held out my free hand, and he wrote a series of

Allyson Lindt

neatly printed letters and numbers on my palm.

"Your password?" Duh. But that felt like important information to just hand someone.

Eli winked. "Pretty sure that means we're going steady, but I won't hold you to it. Use it all until you're done." He pointed me toward his office.

That was it. No questions. No *but we were supposed to go out*.

God, I liked this man.

Fortunately most anything I needed to do could be accessed from any machine. I spent the next few hours on making a dozen phone calls, and having Daria and my assistant make at least as many each.

When I finally wrapped up, it was after eight at night, but our accounts were safe and so were those of the start-up in question. The lot must be empty by now.

I emerged from Eli's office to find the chaotic energy still flowing around me, though it did look like things were wrapping up. Rather than everyone carrying themselves and other things toward the cameras, they were moving things away from the filming area.

I found Eli in the same chair he'd been in when I arrived. He was furiously scribbling notes in a legal pad, and didn't look up when I approached.

"I'm sorry to bail on you like that," I said.

He looked up, and his smile flowed in when his gaze landed on me. "It happens. Is everything fixed?"

"All better." I handed back his computer. "Thank you for this."

"Anytime. You ready to get out of here?"

"Don't you need to finish what you were working on?"

Eli gave a dry laugh and raked his fingers through his hair. "I was waiting on you. The rest is incidental. Take that as you will."

It was both sweet and made me feel bad for wasting his evening.

"Do you still want to go?" He shoved his laptop into a messenger bag, and swung both over his shoulder. "I hear there's a burger place where all the cool kids hang out."

I'd heard the same. The moment Lyndsay found out I was coming out to this small town, that the movie was being filmed here, she told me I *had* to go to Gage's Grub. She'd grown up here, and only recently moved to Salt Lake City.

Xander had backed her up, and since he rarely said anything good about the town his family founded, I figured it must be worth checking out. "I'm in."

"Excellent. My lady." He offered his arm.

It was a little silly and a lot sweet and I didn't hesitate to hook my hand into the crook of his elbow.

We strolled toward the parking lot, but he led us on a path that let us avoid most of the bustling people.

"Do you ever get used to this?" I asked. "The bedlam I mean."

He looked around us, and we turned down a path that ran between trailers and storage containers. "I guess? I don't see it that way, because I grew up in it, so this is what the world is to me."

Even before Donavan? Given his reaction last time I mentioned the show, it wasn't a good idea to bring it up again.

Besides, now I was thinking about Joystick, too. That one incredible night. How I was being almost as impulsive with Eli. But things now felt... safer?

That wasn't the right word. Eli made my heart hammer and my pulse race, and filled my mind with the kind of filthy hope that he'd press me to one of these steel boxes and pick up where we left off yesterday.

"How long have you been in the industry?" I asked. That should be a safe question. "Do people say that? *In the industry*?"

His chuckle was easy and genuine. "People say that. I did my first Oshkosh commercial when I was four."

"Wow." I couldn't imagine parading my son in front of a camera at that age. "I bet you were adorable in the little overalls."

"I could be adorable in little overalls now. If that's your thing?" Eli sounded playful.

I wrinkled my nose. "For the general *aww* factor? Yes. For making out in parking lots, no."

"So making out in parking lots *is* your thing."

"The way you do it, it is." This was easy and fun. "Who's your favorite character you played?"

Eli slipped his hand down to brush mine. It was easy to tangle my fingers with his. The spark was incredible, and at the same time the gesture felt natural.

"Can I go with *me*?" He asked.

Interesting. "Yes, but you have to tell me why."

"None of the fictional ones got to enjoy your company."

Was that sweet or too much? I wasn't sure, but it made my cheeks heat. "That's a bit over the top."

"It's completely sincere." He turned, doing the same for me so we stopped and faced each other. "If you prefer, which answer gets me more of the making out?" He stepped toward me until my back was to a steel box. His body was so close I felt his heat, and temptation spilled through me.

Any of them. As long as I got to feel his lips on mine again. His hands on my body. "You," I said.

"See? And also, Thank God. I'm marginally better in that role than any other." He teased his fingers over my cheek, and the way he searched my face made my heart stop.

"Only marginally?" I teased.

He dragged his thumb over my bottom lip. "I'm an actor. I have to be at least a little good at being someone else."

Fuck me. No, really. I'd let him right here. How

Allyson Lindt

did he do this to me? "Then how do I know the kisses are real?" I kept my tone playful.

"I think you know." He brushed his lips over mine, and I was pretty sure I whimpered. "A brilliant, driven, observant woman like you?" He pressed his mouth in harder, deepening the kiss. "You must know how much I want you." His voice dropped an octave, and the next kiss was enough to curl my toes.

It certainly felt real enough. All of this. I wanted to keep going. There was no reason to stop and move to a more private location, was there? Or to pause for dinner? We could stay here and be naughty and see how much we could get away with, tucked behind storage boxes on a makeshift movie lot?

"Funny meeting you both here." A new voice interrupted the moment.

Was guilt making me hear things? Because I swore to God that sounded like Joystick.

8

joystick

YESTERDAY, when the news about my opening a restaurant hit social media, it wasn't a big deal. Publicity was important and regardless of who had leaked the information, speculation would benefit me.

When I woke up this morning to rumors that I was opening a strip club, that my goal was to corrupt Salt Lake City and bring Hollywood debauchery to town, I changed my mind about wanting this kind of coverage. Local outlets were saying I needed to be stopped. I'd had two real estate appointments cancel on me in the last few hours.

Since then, I'd spent my day doing damage control. Trying to stop the flood of bad press while figuring out where the issue started. On occasion, a site would get a wild hair up their ass and decide to do a *where are they now* kind of piece on me. Those tended to lead to unwanted attention.

This felt different, though. It didn't have a source, and it had grown in a very inorganic way.

If Anonymous wanted to stop me, though, this wasn't the way to do it. I was still determined to plow forward with my project, but now it wasn't just because I wanted it, it was also out of spite.

Half of the work I did was flooding my own social media and that of friends and contacts, with videos and posts of me saying *I'm not opening a strip club anywhere, but when you do see what I've got planned, you're gonna love it.*

Since I wasn't the same kind of name anymore, I didn't keep a PR team on retainer. I preferred handling my own social media anyway.

In the afternoon, my agent called. "Great job on the rebuttals."

"Thanks." I might be friendly with them, but I knew this was a business relationship, and if I looked good, they made more money. Which at least meant they were being sincere in this case. If my response had sucked, I'd be hearing about it.

"I found Elijah."

Hearing those words made my heart flip and a little smile danced on my face. Though, it also made me suspicious. It'd only been a few days since I asked for the favor of tracking Eli down, and even if it only took a few hours to find the information, I expected it to be withheld a lot longer. "Don't keep me in suspense, where is he?"

"He's on set, and it's not a secret or anything, so

you don't have to pretend finding him was a coincidence."

I stared at my phone, hoping to convey my irritation via a look, over the lines, even though we weren't on video. I put the device back to my ear. "Why would I pretend about anything? I'm going to walk onto the set, ask for him, and tell him exactly how I found him."

"Heh. Leave my name out of it." The laughter landed flatly. "And do you think he's going to see you?"

I didn't know, but that wasn't going to stop me from trying. "Give me the information. I'll handle the rest."

An hour later, I was pulling into a makeshift movie lot. The guy working security recognized me —*was a fan from back in the days* in his words—and wanted a selfie.

I was happy to oblige. "I'm here to see Elijah. Could you point me to him?"

His eyes went wide. "Reunion?"

"Something like that." I was hoping exactly like that, but I was already walking a fine line between the honesty I preferred, and pissing him off even further. "But it's a surprise, so do me a favor and keep that pic offline for just half an hour."

"Yeah, of course, man." He pocketed his phone and pointed me in a direction.

I'd gotten here late enough that a lot of the crew was wrapping up for the day. I probably should've waited until tomorrow—it was unlikely Eli was still here—but I had to try *now*. I needed another chance to make things right with him.

Being on set was like coming home, in both bad ways and good. It was easy to wander through the lot toward my destination, and felt natural to take the back path to avoid being stopped too many times for whatever reason.

A familiar voice and a laugh flitted to me, and a shiver of excitement ran through me. *Kandace?*

No. Someone who sounded like her, and I was putting her in their place because she teased my dreams.

"Then how do I know the kisses are real?"

No, that was definitely Kandace. Who was she talking to about kissing? I could step in and provide a personal demonstration and neither she nor they would doubt it was real.

"I think you know."

Fuck. That was Eli. Was it possible for me to be double hard?

"A brilliant, driven, observant woman like you? You must know how much I want you."

He did?

He wasn't an idiot, if he knew her, of course he wanted her. They were both people of good taste. And as I rounded a corner, sure enough, Eli stood toe-to-toe with Kandace, towering over her, kissing her with the kind of intensity that couldn't be acted, no matter how good someone was.

I swore I could feel the heat flowing between them from where I stood, and they had no idea anyone but them existed right now.

They looked sexy as fuck, and I was torn between watching a little longer, and leading with a witty entrance. How did I wittily break up a chemistry-laden staring match between the man I never quite got over and the one night stand I hadn't forgotten?

So you two know each other?

Prettiest sight on the lot.

I was looking for the stars. You must be them.

Ugh.

Eli pressed a hand to Kandace's cheek and drew a thumb over her bottom lip. My dick almost burst through my jeans at the thought of watching the two of them together, but the jealousy was just as intense.

I was about to do something super stupid, I just knew it.

"Funny meeting both of you here," I said.

As if the master himself, John Woo, was shooting the scene, the entire world slowed to a crawl as both of them turned to me. Eli's scowl flowed in like an art form, and pink spread across Kandace's cheeks.

"Both? Wait, you know him?" The world was back to normal speed as Eli glanced at Kandace.

She shrugged. "We've met. I wouldn't say we *know* each other."

In the biblical sense.

"You didn't think to mention it." It was hard to tell if Eli was hurt or angry.

"You were very insistent we not talk about him," Kandace sounded matter of fact. "And it wasn't as though I expected to see him again. It was one night in Italy." She snapped her jaw shut and her blush grew.

Her words could mean a lot of things, but her reaction to them carried a heavy implication.

Was I smug? Disappointed? Not the second one. Not at all. I could swoop in and rescue Kandace from the man who wouldn't let her talk about her past, but I was that past, and I was here to see him.

It's not a big deal. There's no way this is the first time we've slept with the same person. I'm sure you were fine, Eli. That could be fun, but it was mean and counterproductive. I really didn't want Eli walking away again.

"It seems like we all have a lot to talk about," I said. "I drove past a burger place on my way into town. Buy you both dinner?"

Was I crashing their date?

Probably.

Was I going to do it anyway?

Definitely.

9

joystick

I WAS surprised that Kandace and Eli agreed to dinner, especially him. When he added, "Maybe this will get you to go away," that was more like it.

I doubted I would, but we'd see how the night went. Once all three of us talked, and Eli and I got past the animosity, I could move forward. Though I'd been here to apologize to him, and make the past right, seeing him with Kandace made me realize how much I wanted them both. Together would be ideal, but separately would work if I had to settle.

Gage's Grub was packed. Saturday night, at the only burger joint in town, I wasn't surprised. It was too loud for conversation while we waited in line, and I hoped we'd be able to talk once we sat down.

We placed our order, and I handed over my credit card before Eli could pay. His brow furrowed in response. A large section of photo, the kind of strip that came out of those booths they used to have in the malls, slipped into view in my wallet, and I tucked it away again, before Eli could see and make whatever assumptions he was going to make.

"Can I get a name?" The girl behind the register asked.

She was probably about the same age Eli and I had been when we were split apart, all those years ago.

"*Donovan*," someone shouted.

And I was pretty sure Eli's scowl was testing the theory of *if you hold an expression too long it'll freeze that way*. I turned toward the shout, to see a man in his early twenties waving at me.

"It's you, isn't it?" His jaw dropped and his eyes grew wide. "Holy crap, it's both of you."

My smile came easily, the reaction having been ingrained in me since childhood. Who was I kidding? I loved the attention, but I doubted my dinner companions would. "It is."

"No. Way." He tapped the arm of the woman with him. "Dude, *dude*."

"I see." She was staring at us with a similar expression to her friend's.

He shoved his phone at her. "Take a picture. Can I take a picture with you? Take a picture."

"Sure." I kept my body language open, while trying not to disrupt everyone around us.

It didn't matter. Chaos unfurled in seconds, when people realized a celebrity was here. People were pushing in, getting pushed out, and questions were flying.

"Are you here for the movie?"

"Are you both in it?"

Eli scowled more and more between each picture. But he managed a smile while the cameras were pointed at us.

"Who's she?"

"Can we take a picture with you?"

Kandace faded further back into the throngs of people.

"Is that really Elijah?"

"How come you don't act anymore?"

This wasn't what I was here for, and I needed to shut it down now.

"Did the two of you really used to f—"

"Come on, guys." A booming voice cut over the noise, and the glut of people seemed to part like Charlton Heston with the Red Sea. "They're here for burgers, just like the rest of you. Give them some room." The man who approached had dark hair, and the kind of muscles and growly expression that would make him the next new and hot thing in Hollywood action movies.

His used-to-be-white *Kiss the Cook* apron would probably make him the next Jean Claude Van Damme. "Break it up. Let them get their food," he shouted.

The crowd fell back, though most of the eyes were still on us. "We should get this to go," I said quietly, so only Eli and Kandace should hear me.

And this man. He gave a quick shake of his head.

"Wouldn't hear of it." He turned to the cashier. "Is this their food?"

"Yes."

He grabbed two trays, one with burgers and fries and one with shakes, and balanced both as if it was the most natural thing in the world. "Come on." He jerked his head toward the back of the restaurant.

We followed him through a door that led to a half-lit room, and two walls of booths. He set our trays on one of the tables that ran down the middle.

"I'm Gage, and I'm sorry about that."

Like on the sign. Cool. I shook his hand. "Joy-stick." I jerked my thumb at myself. "Kandace, and Elijah."

"Eli, please." He corrected me. "Thank you, for out there."

Gage waved a hand. "Don't mention it. Feel free to stay back here as long as you want. Knock on the door over there if you need anything, and one of my crew will get it for you."

"Thank you. Seriously."

"I do have a favor to ask in return," Gage said.

Here it came. "What's that?"

"Are you with the movie crew that's here?"

Eli stepped forward. "I am."

"Their caterer is making a series of Southwest dishes that the cast keeps raving about, and I'd love to pick the cook's brain about what they're doing."

"I'll do whatever I can," Eli said.

Gage left us to eat, and we settled at the table. It

was probably a good thing we didn't pick a booth, because I would've wanted to sit next to both Kandace and Eli, and wouldn't have been able to pick either.

"What happened to your thumb?" I asked Eli as we started eating. I was certain it hadn't been in a splint when I picked him up.

Kandace was cutting into her burger with a plastic knife and fork I hadn't seen her grab. "He saved me from an angry mic." She managed demure but assertive at the same time. To look neat and tidy while eating one of the messiest hamburgers I'd ever seen.

I did love watching her.

"He's good at that. Sacrificing himself." I meant it. One of the things I remembered fondly about Eli is how he was always there for anyone who needed him.

"Even if the other person supposedly doesn't know it." The edge in Eli's voice was distinct and sharp. "Hell, I did it for Austin's career."

If I'd known that at the time, I never would have let him. Any chance we could fight through it, and get it out of the way? "Why would I have assumed that? My staff told me a story, and I had no reason to think otherwise at the time." I'd been so *adorably* naive.

"Because I told you how I felt. Because why would I just go without a word?" Eli gave me a look of intense disbelief.

It was hard to answer the question from my perspective then, knowing what I did now, but I would try. "I thought you thought the sex was bad." Or rather, I thought he'd figured out we just weren't going to work together.

"We were kids. Who'd never done it before. Of course the sex was bad. I didn't know any better. And then when they told me…" Eli clenched his jaw and scrubbed his face.

They told him I wanted to do the show alone. That I said I was better without him next to me. Those lying fucking assholes made him thing that I wanted him off the set. I could see how that would fuck a guy up. I didn't know at the time he'd been told any of that, because those words had never come from me. When I found out, much later, I'd been furious. By then, it was too late. Eli was done with me, with taking my calls, with all of it. "I didn't say any of the things they told you I did."

"I didn't know that at the time." His voice went quiet.

Yeah, well, "You never even tried to call me. To confirm."

"I tried. Over and over. Every time I was near a phone, I tried to call and ask you why you hated me. They only ever told me you wouldn't take my calls."

"Would you like me to come back, so the two of you can talk?" Kandace asked.

We both reached for her at the same time, with overlapping *Nos*.

"Please, don't." Eli got to the rest of his sentence first. "I'd much rather your company than his."

"I'd rather be spending the evening with both of you," I added. "And I'm sorry, Elijah. I really, truly am." And I had been for years. He never deserved what they did to him on my behalf.

He sighed. "Yeah, well sorry doesn't fix what fifteen years of therapy hasn't touched."

Swell. Not.

We went back to our burgers, with an awkward silence settling into the room. When a loud chirp penetrated the lack of conversation, we all jumped.

Kandace reached for her phone with a frown. "I'm sorry, it's my son. I need to take this." Her chair screeched on tile when she pushed back from the table, and she wandered away as she answered.

"I don't know why you still carry that thing in your wallet." Eli's comment caught me off-guard.

Ah. He'd seen it after all. "Carry what?" Ridiculous for me to pretend, but it wasn't as though my being sentimental would crack his shell.

He almost smiled, but it didn't reach his eyes, and it didn't look pleasant. "The photos in your wallet. The ones we took at that stupid photo booth they brought on set for episode 372."

"Are you really so jaded that every one of your memories is bad?" I wanted his forgiveness, but this... "It wasn't stupid. It was one of the best days I ever had on set." Because I didn't get to go to the mall as a normal kid growing up, and for a few days, that changed. Sure, it was all fake, but I could pretend.

And Eli and I had to do so many takes in that

photo booth. Making goofy faces. Figuring out how to fit both of us in there.

"It *was* stupid. Because they didn't put film in it until the end, so you have the only photos," Eli said.

Did he just... I wasn't going to make a big deal out of the fact that he just showed a hint of something other than grumpiness. "It's a strip of four. Do you want two?"

"I'm sorry about that," Kandace said as she pushed through the door leading from the kitchen, holding three beer bottles by the necks. She paused a few feet away and looked between us. "Did I interrupt? Do you want me to come back?"

Yes, but also no. "We're good," I said at the same time Eli said, "Don't go."

I should've said that. So much better. This was why he was the script fixer. "Is everything all right?" I asked as Kandace sat a drink in front of each of us and sat down. "Or has something tonight driven you to drink?"

She gave a light laugh. "The beer is from Gage. He says it's on the house as an apology. I also get the impression he wouldn't be offended if we were to mention his microbrewery to friends and fans if we enjoy it, but he didn't say that. The call was an out, in case I needed it."

"An out?" Eli repeated.

"If the date wasn't going well."

So this had been a date, and I crashed it. Though,

neither of them told me *no*. "You must have a good relationship with your son."

Kandace gave a brief nod. "I do. He's the best kid in the world, even if he's technically not a kid anymore."

Like that, I adored her more. Growing up, it had just been Mom and me. And an entire TV cast and crew, of course. And Eli. But Mom was my biggest fan. Between her and the way my TV family was scripted, I thought the world was all rainbows and unicorns for everyone's families.

When I lost her, I was devastated. And when I realized so many families were nothing like ours, I learned to appreciate Mom—and every parent who had a respectful, loving relationship with their children—so much more.

"You came back, so it must not be too bad." Like that, Eli's demeanor had shifted. He was no longer grumpy and scorned, but he was sweet and smitten.

"It's a night I'll never forget," Kandace said.

That could be good or bad, but I was going to assume good given that she hadn't bailed with the phone call.

I sipped the beer, then took another, longer drink. It was actually pretty good.

"Can I ask you both something?" Though Kandace's tone was polite, there was no deference in her voice. None of the shyness I'd seen in Italy.

Something told me I was about to see a woman who was a partner in a multi-billion dollar investment firm, rather than the one who was uncertain about things like one-night stands. "Of course," I said.

"I know you asked me not to bring this up, Eli, but no one can miss the tension between you two, and there are dozens of rumors out there, and if we're going to keep—" She paused and took a deep breath. "What are you two to each other?"

What does that make us?

Absolutely nothing.

Thanks, *Spaceballs*.

Yes, I was here to make things right with Eli, nothing more. And seeing Kandace again was a bonus.

But I didn't want to give her *we're nothing to each other* answer, despite the fact that it was true, and was probably what she needed to hear to let either of us continue pursuing her.

10
elijah

WHY DID I agree to let Austin come to dinner with us? What was wrong with me?

And now Kandace was asking the one question I knew was going to come up again, but I'd still hoped to avoid... for the rest of my life.

What are you two to each other?

Since we were here, I was going to tell the truth before we had to hear Austin's version instead. "We were actually best friends when we were kids." That hurt far more to say than I expected. "We became more, and when the people at the top realized their TV sweetheart, Donovan, might be gay, and that news might get out, they fired me."

Austin winced.

"I'm so sorry," Kandace frowned.

I shrugged. "It was a long time ago. As for what we are to each other now? Nothing." Did I manage to say that without any emotion? I hoped so.

"It couldn't have been all bad, or you wouldn't have been together, even when you were younger," Kandace said.

What was she doing—trying to breathe life into a decades' old relationship? Nothing about this night was like a normal date. I'd love to blame that on Austin showing up, but I was fooling myself if I thought any bit of this relationship was *normal*.

Which was why I was here. Because Kandace was different. And she was probably trying to make an awkward evening less awkward.

"I didn't think it was all bad." Austin replied while I was still stuck in my own head.

"It wasn't," I agreed. "Is this what we want to get into tonight?"

Kandace nibbled on her fries and washed the food down with a swallow of beer. "It wouldn't have been my first choice, but here we are. My son says..." She gave a brief shake of her head. "You have to know what the fan theories are about the two of you."

I did. "That we were secret lovers."

"That we still are," Austin said.

"That I'm his housewife and no one knows because shh... Secret." I pressed my finger to my lips.

The way Austin chuckled, like it was easy, like this was the kind of situation he found himself in every day, set my teeth on edge. "Eli would make a terrible housewife."

Kandace raised her brows. "I've seen his office. I have a hard time believing that."

"Not because I'm bad at it." I wasn't letting the blame fall on me.

Austin shook his head. "Not at all. But I'm horrible at being told where to put things and the instant I didn't do it the way Eli said—"

"I'd let him know. If we weren't already on the outs, that'd do it." I couldn't imagine being married to Austin. Not even for a second. Never had.

Maybe for a little while I had.

Kandace laughed. Not the reaction I expected.

"This was what I was about to bring up," she said. "So many anything-but-straight kinds, especially young boys, especially my son who struggled so much with his sexuality when he was younger, saw your show. They saw the chemistry the two of you had. Even if you weren't allowed to express it back then, you both changed their worlds."

I'd seen the various fan theories over the years, about my relationship with Austin. I know what kind of popularity the show had now. But I'd never heard someone personally say something like I'd changed their world. How was I supposed to react?

"That chemistry didn't exist without there being something between the two of you. Don't tell me it was all bad."

We'd already agreed it wasn't, right? Which was why flashing back to those moments that were good with Austin hurt.

He knocked back the rest of his beer, and set the bottle on the table with a solid *thud*. "Remember the night we discovered someone on set was keeping real beer in the set fridge?"

"Oh, God." I did. Vividly. "That was such a mistake" I took a sip of my own drink, hoping it would loosen some of the tension in my neck.

"Don't keep me in suspense, tell me the rest of the story." Kandace leaned in, curiosity sparkling in her eyes.

Austin jerked his head at me. "Eli's the storyteller."

Seriously? "We sneaked the beer out of the fridge, we got drunk, and it was a disaster."

"Really?" Kandace twisted her mouth in amusement. "This is what my brother pays you for?" Her tone was playful. "We're all here; we might as well make the evening fun. Tell me the story."

How was I supposed to turn down a request like that? The past tugged at my heart, and it hurt, so I might as well remember the fun bits too. "The guy who was bringing the booze in drank one of those brands that came with the screw off tops. We thought we were being clever. Austin and I would each drink half a bottle, fill them up with water, and then put them back. We figured no one would ever know."

I wished I didn't remember that with so much fondness. But I had a soft spot for a lot of Austin's stupid schemes. Back then I'd been so jealous I wasn't the one to come up with them first.

"How long did it take before you got caught?" Kandace looked captivated.

"I'm pretty sure he knew Day One," I said. "He let us get away with it for about a week. One of the shoots was really stressful, and Austin and I were going to be adults and drink *all* the beer. Because that must be smart, right?"

Damn it, now I was remembering more of what went on that night, and almost having fun with the past, and I didn't want that. "We were lucky the guy the beer belonged to—it was one of the ADs, was the same person who found us. We were sick and pretty much passed out."

"I was terrified he was going to tell my mom," Austin added. "I came clean to her the next day, and begged for her forgiveness."

The AD said we'd learned our lesson and we'd keep it between us. "You're lucky she didn't tell anyone else."

"I begged her not to get you in trouble." The sincerity in Austin's retort made my breath catch.

I knew that at the time, but the reminder… "The AD made us keychains out of the bottle caps. To remind us not to be idiots again. I still have mine." For far smarter reasons than nostalgia.

"No." Austin sounded like he didn't believe me.

"Yes. To remind me your schemes never worked out, and to not be an idiot again. It hangs on the inside of my briefcase."

"That's kind of sweet," Kandace said.

Austin scoffed. "That's kind of unbelievable."

I would *not* be called a liar. Especially not by him. I

finished my beer and let the alcohol settle in enough to numb the bad parts of the past. "Do you want to see? It's back at the hotel."

"Did you just invite me back to your room?" Austin teased.

"You really did." Kandace didn't look like she minded.

Pft. Whatever. "Is that a *no* on seeing proof?"

"I didn't say that."

I looked at Kandace. "You wouldn't leave the two of us alone, would you?" I had no idea how this roller coaster was careening out of control, but I wanted her with me on it.

"Hell no, I wouldn't." Kandace grinned. "This story is too good for me to walk away now."

This was ridiculous. But also... a little fun? Austin had to know I wasn't lying about the keychain, but we were all going to trek back to my temporary home regardless, to stare at a tiny little object from our past?

The part of my saying *sure, why not*? Must be way more drunk than the rest of me.

We finished up our dinner, thanked Gage for the meal and the privacy, and thanked him again when he let us out the back, so we could avoid the crowds. I almost felt like a kid again, sneaking behind buildings with Austin, to get away. Back then it could have been from the fans, or from the set, or any other number of ridiculous things.

And tonight, Kandace seemed to be enjoying the

ride along with us. Her smile and light laugh were infectious.

We decided to walk, as I was only staying a few blocks away and going on foot might be faster and easier than trying to get back to the car.

"Is this where you grew up?" Austin asked Kandace as we strolled down the street.

An odd sort of envy spiked through me that he had a reason to ask her that question. I hadn't done so because I knew the answer, from Andrew. When she shook her head, I realized she was going to tell the story in a very different way.

"No," she said. "The place we actually grew up is nearly an hour away. It looked a lot like this, though. Maybe more run-down." She scrunched up her face. "*Definitely* more run down. But they didn't want to be associated with his name, and this place has a… more flexible city council."

"Your hometown didn't want to be known as *The Town that Birthed Internet Porn*?" Austin spread his hands across the air in front of him.

Kandace laughed. "Pretty sure that's a type of porn itself. Rule 34, right?"

"That's kind of meta." Now I was trying to wrap my brain around an actual location giving birth and… I needed to stop that.

"And I hate to break it to both of you, but Andrew didn't invent internet porn, he just figured out how to make money from it. Nude photos have been online longer than AOL."

The look of confusion that crossed Austin's face was the same kind of exaggerated expression he would feed the camera when we were kids. One of those looks that made his TV parents, and fans, and everyone go *Oh, Donovan,* with the *wah-wah* sound implied. "AO-what?"

"Do *not* make me feel old like that." Kandace managed both teasing and warning in the same tone.

"He's yanking your chain. We used to play on AOL all the time. They sponsored the show." Was this me being the hero? I had no idea anymore. Could I possibly stop overthinking the situation long enough to have fun? Did I want to let my guard down like that around Austin? For Kandace I did.

"So the episode where Eli—your character—was addicted to computer games, was that based on reality?" Kandace glanced at me.

She knew our episodes.

"Do you remember how the episode ended?" I asked.

Kandace ducked her head. "I never paid attention to most of them. I just caught enough to have an idea that they weren't corrupting Lucas."

They might have been, though not in the way some people thought. "It ends with Donovan confronting me with all our parents, and us agreeing that even though I spent too much time gaming, the computer, and the internet, weren't inherently bad. That I could learn so many things from being online."

Austin did the hand-wipe across the sky thing

again. *"Brought to you by AOL. Welcome to the World Wide Wow."*

"God, I'd almost forgotten how tacky that was." I laughed with embarrassment. "But in answer to your question, no. That wasn't based on me. I'm not sure if I'm offended or flattered that the geeky episode would be centered on my sins."

Kandace laughed again. "Were any of them based on reality? You probably get that question a lot."

"Not really." Austin turned so he could face us, and walked backwards. Somehow he managed to do so without running into anything behind him.

This answer was more my realm than his, at least these days. "The old Hollywood writers, the ones who have been around forever, know which tropes and episodes work. You stick someone new in the writers' room, and in approximately two-point-seven days, they've been assimilated into *this is the way we've always done it*. The tropes, the jokes, and all of it."

"Two-point-seven?" Kandace repeated. "Anyone ever make it to three?"

"Not once. Two-point-eight-nine is the record." I spoke with mock authority. "Hell, I've been assimilated seventy-nine times this month."

Austin snorted. "Would've been funnier if you said sixty-nine."

I faked a horrified-but-half-assed scream. "They've gotten to you." I grabbed him by the shoulders, jerking us both to a stop, and shook him. "Don't go into the light. The camera light. Watch out, you're heading straight for a drug addiction that can be resolved in twenty-four minutes, including intervention and character self-actualization."

"Ahh." Austin threw his hands over his face and crumbled to his knees. "I can't stop. They help me diet-stay-awake-ease-the-pain-of-break-up-look-popular. Help me..." He collapsed further into himself.

People murmured and stepped around us on the sidewalk. All two of them. Across the street, someone had their phone out and pointed toward us.

Kandace was blushing red, but her smile was unmistakable. "I have a feeling I won't be able to go in public with the two of you in the future."

The two of you. Nope. This was my date with her. Not his. Not ours. I wrapped an arm around her waist. "Not a problem. We'll ditch the drama queen and go have fun."

"*You* said I could join you." Austin climbed to his feet. "Besides, I still need to see this mysterious keychain I don't think really exists."

Once we did that, I could send him on his way and pretend I wasn't almost having fun out here. I gestured toward the house we stood in front of. "They turned this into a boarding house for the crew. My room is in here."

Like that, the mood fell flat. I wasn't sure if I was pleased with myself or disappointed.

Definitely disappointed, as much as I didn't want

to admit it. There was no conversation as I unlocked my room door and let us in. The place was basically a studio apartment, with a bed, a cute little kitchenette, and a bathroom big enough for a shower and a toilet.

I didn't need more.

I tugged my briefcase from its spot, set it on the desk, and opened it to reveal the keychain dangling from it. The lamplight glinted off the bottle cap, and a pit of nostalgia and longing settled into my gut. "There it is. Proof. Happy?" I closed the case again, before I could start to catch feels.

"Yeah." Austin's tone was flat.

Wow, things were awkward in here. I lingered near the bed, Austin was a few feet away, and Kandace stood by the kitchen counter, arms folded and gaze turned on her feet.

Now what?

11
kandace

THIS WASN'T what I expected from my evening. Hell, I'd packed an overnight back, fully hoping to spend the night naked in bed with Eli.

Instead, I felt like I should step in and play peacemaker. These men obviously had a painful history—they said as much—but even if they hadn't told me, it would be obvious. They were each hurting in different ways. The friend in me wanted to help and the businesswoman in me felt compelled to mediate.

At least I wasn't torn about what to do. I may have never expected to see Joystick again, but he was a lot of fun to spend time with and *really* good in bed and I hated to see him hurt.

When it came to Eli, I'd love to have an actual date with him, and something told me the two of them needed to get past this for that to happen. Besides, was it so wrong that I wanted a taste of both of them? If I went to a bakery, I was an adult, I could have two cookies. Why did I have to take a side and pick just one guy? Especially without a sample of each.

"That night you got really drunk." I was going to take us back to the topic they seemed to connect on. I liked knowing more about them, and hated talking about myself and my past. Besides, Andrew was about to air a lot of my dirty laundry for the world to see. Soon, everyone would think they knew me. "What else did you do besides get caught?"

They both paled and exchanged furtive glances.

"Do you remember?" I nudged playfully. It was clear they did at least a little.

Eli winced. Every time he did that, his nose scrunched up and his serious expression turned adorable. He'd probably hate hearing that—most men didn't like to be called adorable by their dates, I was sure—but it also made him vulnerable and kissable.

God, those kisses…

"We went out on the town," Joystick said.

Eli's wince grew. "—ish. We went out on the town-ish. We weren't old enough to know what that really meant, and we went to the nearest convenience store and tried to buy more beer. Both for ourselves and to replace what we drank."

Joystick let out a barking laugh. "The guy behind the counter didn't believe for a second that we were old enough."

"Especially since he recognized us right away, and threatened to leak the security footage to the press if we didn't scram." Eli's smile was almost back. If he wasn't careful, it might burst through. "So we scrammed. Went to another place, and decided we were more hungry than anything."

"Those hot dogs..." Joystick pulled a disgusted face. "They looked so sus. What was it you said?"

Eli held up his hands and shook his head. "I didn't say anything. Except maybe, *Austin, we should go.*" His laugh slipped out.

"Liar." The way Joystick pointed, his tone, were both comically exaggerated. "What you said was *how long do you think a guy has to jerk off before his wiener looks like that?*"

"It was wordplay—wiener, hot dog, dick..."

"Ha." Joystick looked smug. "So you admit you said it."

Eli let out a long sigh. "Yeah, fine. I said it. But at least I didn't say *we should get a couple. See how they taste.*"

Joystick cringed. "And I was wrong." This wasn't the smooth-talking guy who took me back to the hotel in Italy. He looked the same. Sounded the same. But he was more relaxed and more himself.

I could almost see them having the conversation now. Eli trying to be smart. Reasonable. Joystick knowing better but egging him on anyway. Years apart, and that connection between them still existed. Did they know that? Would they admit it?

And God, I wanted them both. Was that wrong? It had to be. Everything about the way I was raised said it was wrong. Yeah, sure, I knew multiple people who were in three-person relationships, but I wasn't wild and free Kandace.

I wanted to be. And I wanted to be watching the two of them kissing, and—

"Are you all right?" Eli was looking at me.

"Fine. Why?"

He tilted his head to study me. "You're making a face and blushing."

"She's thinking about wieners," Joystick offered.

My cheeks grew hotter. I could deny it, but I didn't think the lie would come out believable. Besides, it wasn't right to lie. "Was your relationship really so bad that it's made you bitter for more than a decade?" I'd already asked something similar, but my brain was stalled on the two of them kissing, and I couldn't make new thoughts.

"I'm not bitter." Joystick almost sounded sincere.

Eli shrugged. "Me neither."

I raised my eyebrows in disbelief.

"I just thought the boy I loved had decided I wasn't worth loving back, and walked away," Joystick said.

Eli clenched his jaw. "You left me."

"I never went anywhere. I tried to follow you, and you shut me out."

"I thought you'd discarded me." Hurt slithered its way into Eli's retort.

"And now you know better, and you're still shutting me out."

I was watching a television drama play out in real

life. It wasn't fun, and I hated that they were both hurt this way. What was I doing thinking about dating—fucking—one or both of them? I was already at a point where I didn't know who I'd pick if I had to, and I'd become another thing between them if they asked me to. "I should let the two of you talk."

"No." Eli stepped in my path as I reached for the door. "Austin should go. I'm still the same guy I was before he showed up, and I want to spend my evening with *you*."

"Besides, if you go, he'll blame me and we'll fight again. At least if I leave now, I get to walk out on a higher note than when I arrived. Or at least not a lower one." Joystick didn't try to hide his bitterness.

Eli jammed his hands in his pockets. "It's not like we're going to kiss and make up."

This wasn't a convincing argument from either of them, but I didn't really want to go. I felt like I should. Like if I were thinking clearly, it would be the right thing to do. Instead, I wanted to stay and watch this *make up* kiss.

"Why not?" Joystick asked.

Yeah, why not?

Damn my body, heating up at the thought of this spat turning hotter. Turning physical. Was hate fucking a thing? I didn't want that.

Did I?

If it was hot, and between these two—

Stop, me.

"Because we're not... I mean... You're not my date

for the night." Eli fumbled with his answer to Joystick's question. Eli moved back into the room, putting him face to face with Joystick.

I couldn't help but turn and watch.

"Not sure what that has to do with making up," Joystick said.

Eli let out an exasperated huff. "It has everything to do with kissing. It's in the phrase—*kiss and make up*."

"You're going to tell me you *never* wonder if there's still a spark between us? You never wonder if we would still be together or could get together again?" Joystick's tone was half-taunting, half-hopeful.

Eli scowled. "*Never* is an all-inclusive phrase. It doesn't leave any room for interpretation, and there are always exceptions..."

My skin was on fire from the heat and tension in the room. It didn't matter if my reaction was wrong or right, because it was real. My pulse raced and I wanted to look away, but I also wanted things to turn as sexy as possible. If I breathed wrong, I might ruin the balance in here.

"Do you?" Joystick pushed. "Do you ever wonder if there's still a spark?"

"Yes." Eep. I didn't mean to say that out loud.

One corner of Joystick's mouth tugged up, but he kept his gaze on Eli, who stared back at him intently.

"Fine." Eli took another step toward Joystick. "If we do this, can we move on?" He gripped the back of Joystick's neck and crushed their mouths together.

Oh wow.

Joystick shifted the power, taking control of the kiss and drawing the moment out until I felt it in my toes. In my fingers and nipples. God, I wanted to be a part of that sandwich.

This was where I should leave. Actually go before the room combusted from the heat sparking between them.

But I didn't want to turn away. I wanted them to keep going, and I wanted to watch every freaking minute of it.

12

joystick

KISSING ELI WAS SUCH a bad idea. Now that I'd started, I didn't want to stop this incredible, hungry moment.

I was intently aware that Kandace watched us. I should feel bad about doing this in front of her, but I got the impression she didn't mind, and I did love an audience.

Fuck, I missed this. But this kiss was so much better than when we were kids. We knew what we were doing. Eli's body pressed to mine was hard and unyielding. My dick was so hard I swore I was carrying forged steel in my pants. I should pause at least long enough to make sure this was all good.

I made myself nudge Eli back, and Kandace's soft whimper gripped my shaft like an invisible fist.

"We should..." I couldn't get the word *stop* out.

"Remember back then?" Eli's statement was open-ended and vague. It could mean so many things.

And I knew exactly which one he was talking about, because it was how the hot dog incident ended. "We went back to my trailer."

"You asked me if my dick really looked like a hot dog after I jerked off, and I told you of course not," Eli said.

We'd been so drunk, the entire thing could've been an episode of Donovan about consent. It didn't matter to either of us back then. "I told you to prove it."

"And I said I would if you did."

"Did you really... you know?" Kandace looked enthralled. Pink cheeks. Swollen, kissable lips. So fuckable. Hell, I even wanted to cuddle after.

I nodded in response to her question. "It was the first time we jerked off in front of each other. We promised no touching, no kissing, just watching. That way it wasn't weird."

I expected Kandace to say *I should go*, but she stepped further into the room. "Don't stop on my account. I could watch." Her voice grew shy. "No kissing, no touching, and that way it's not weird."

This was bad. Or good. Or... "Tell me to stop, Eli. Tell me to go. Tell me something."

"Don't go." Eli grabbed my shirt and kissed me again.

The heat that flowed between us and swirled around us was blistering, and our lips and tongues danced, the more of the past floated to the surface. So many feelings I thought I'd left behind. I needed to taste more of him. To feel as much of Eli as I could.

I traveled my mouth along his jaw, savoring the scruff of five o'clock shadow, and nipping at his neck as I moved lower.

Out of the corner of my eye, I saw Kandace lower herself into a chair. Her gaze was fixed on us, her lips and legs both parted slightly.

Yummy. I sank my teeth into Eli's shoulder, drawing a grunt, and dragged a teasing thumb over one of his nipples, though his shirt. I didn't know what we were doing, just that I needed it to keep going.

I slid both hands to his ass, gripping hard and pressing my body into his until his erection dug into my hip.

The kiss became a free-for-all of groping and stroking. It felt so good to have his hands on me. To touch him.

I needed more, though. I undid Eli's belt and slid down his zipper.

"What are you doing?" His question was breathy and curious, rather than cold and demanding.

I slid my body down his, until I was on my knees at his feet, then looked up to meet his gaze. "Apologizing."

Kandace sighed.

My dick was going to drill a hole through my pants any minute now. But I had other priorities. I freed Eli, relishing his groan as I drew him into my mouth. The desperation in the air made every movement feel frantic, from dragging my tongue along

Eli's shaft to fumbling one-handed with my own jeans, to free my dick.

Kandace slipped her hand down her pants, and kept her half-lidded gaze on us. Her chest rose and fell quickly with her needy breaths.

Having her as an audience, tasting Eli, jerking myself off, was a trifecta of perfection.

I dove into pleasuring Eli. Stroking, licking, taking as much of him as I could without gagging. Each time he thrust into my mouth, I relished the exchange. When the jerk of his hips grew faster, when his restraint slipped, I picked up my speed as well and moved my other hand to finger his sac.

The only warning I had was a pause in Eli's grunts, and a shudder, before he spilled his load down the back of my throat. I loved the way he tasted, filling my mouth while my own erection hung free, waiting for attention.

The incredible sounds Kandace was making said she was coming too. I lost myself in both, still licking Eli, until he shuddered away from my touch, and slipped out past my lips.

He sank to his knees next to me, grabbed my hand, and used both our grips to fist my cock. This was nothing like before. There was no uncertainty or hesitation. We both wanted—needed—this.

His grip was tight around mine, almost too much, but also not enough. I lost myself in the sensation of the two of us jerking me off. I was already so turned on, so close thanks to Kandace and Eli's pleasures, that it didn't take much to draw me to orgasm.

My entire body tensed as I came, and I felt the shudder of release spill from me. I didn't care that the mess got all over my clothes. The only thing that mattered was how incredible it felt being those close to Eli again. Having Kandace here watching us.

A tiny voice in the back of my head reminded me this wasn't a long-term deal. Not for either of them. Not for me.

That didn't mean I had to stop enjoying the moment. In fact, it was the biggest reason to make the most of this.

"There weren't any hotdogs at the convenience store that were pierced." Eli's voice was lighter. More playful.

I liked that. "Mine's also not overcooked, or up for sale to anyone who walks in."

"I should clean up a little." Light glistened off Kandace's sticky, slick fingers as she stood.

Yummy.

"Wait." Eli extracted himself from our two-person pile, his half-hard dick hanging out. He grabbed Kandace's wrist. "Austin's gotten to taste you and I haven't." He drew two of her fingers into his mouth, and sucked them slowly.

She groaned as he licked her clean.

Should I be ready to go again already? Because *fuck* that was hot.

When Eli finished, he pressed his mouth to Kandace's. So much for not kissing. Not that I minded. A dangerous blend of lust and jealousy spilled inside, and I couldn't fight either.

Eli finally let go. "Now you should go clean up."

Kandace's playful smirk was worth a million bucks, and she vanished into the bathroom.

I forced myself to my feet as well. "I should take a hint from her. Change my clothes... or something?" Cum stained my shirt and splattered the front of my jeans.

"That's that?" Eli asked. "You just jerk and squirt and run?"

"As opposed to...?" I didn't want to go.

The bathroom door was open a crack. "We could call Gage. See if he'll send over some more of that beer." Kandace's suggestion floated out.

That sounded like a bad idea.

I was so in.

WHEN I WOKE UP, my head was pounding. My foot hurt too. Not a lot, but it was the kind of ache that made me think it would be worse in a few hours. It was bright in here. I could tell without opening my eyes. And loud.

What happened?

I'd been in Eli's room. With him and Kandace. The lighting wasn't so harsh in there. *Fuck* my foot hurt.

I forced my eyes open.

"Hey." A bleary-eyed Kandace smiled at me.

The setting was wrong. Sound stage?

Hospital.

"Why are we in a hospital?" I asked.

13
elijah

WHEN AUSTIN HAD CALLED GAGE, we quickly found ourselves in possession of twelve bottles of beer, in four different flavors. And we'd had to try them all.

We didn't get blindingly drunk, not so much I'd forgotten any of what happened, but we were pretty far gone.

And as I watched Austin process the last few hours, and recognition spread across his face, I knew he'd just remembered too.

"Oh." He pressed a palm to his forehead.

I suspected he was in a bit of pain, between his ankle and everything else. The doctor refused to give him anything stronger than acetaminophen, because he was drunk. "Yeah, oh." I didn't know what else to say.

"I'll grab the doctor." Kandace stepped from the room.

I should have volunteered to do that. It wasn't as though I had anything to say to Austin.

We'd decided to go for a walk when we were each about three beers in. The town was quiet that time of night, which gave it a whole new vibe. A peaceful-but-eerie kind of feeling. We'd ended up at the park, where I pushed Kandace on the swings until we were all giggling.

And then I wanted to climb on *the big climby thingy with bars and wood.*

Cue the drunken jokes about wood. Kandace had corrected me, and told me it was a jungle gym, which gave Austin an excuse to tease me for not knowing everything after all. He'd also pointed out I couldn't swing on the horizontal bars very well, because I had a broken thumb.

Didn't matter. I wanted to go anyway. Now that I was several cups of hospital coffee into sobriety, I could look back on the decision and see what an idiot Drunk Eli was. He'd been convinced that he could impress Kandace that way. That Austin was winning, and I just needed to prove I was big and strong.

Fucking Drunk Eli.

Austin was helpful, though. He held my legs while I swung across the bars. It was going great until I slipped and he slipped and we tumbled down with me landing on top of him. Which was when he snapped his ankle.

"I'm sorry," I said.

He grinned. "Totally worth it."

What? "No it wasn't. You've got a broken bone because I was a drunken moron."

"And it hurts like fuck. But I made my choices. Besides, sometimes you need people looking out for you. You don't always have to be the strong one."

Seriously? He was lying in bed, in obvious pain, and he was being cool about it. I couldn't hate him. I couldn't forgive him. I felt horrible about what happened regardless of his assurance.

Fuck.

Kandace returned with the doctor, who spent a few minutes checking Austin's foot and asking a series of questions about pain, mobility, and who would be staying with him for the next two to four weeks, while he needed to keep his weight off his foot.

"I'm from out of town—"

"He's staying with me." I talked over Austin. This was my fault, and it was up to me to make it right.

Austin stared at me, and for the first time since he'd walked back into my life, I swore he was completely out of words.

"Great." The doctor made a few more notes on his tablet, then dropped it in a coat pocket. "We'll schedule a follow-up for you, to discuss if surgery is needed. And, I'm sorry to ask but my daughter is a huge fan. Could I…?"

"Selfie? Autograph? Of course." There was Austin again.

While Austin was being discharged, I called an

Uber for us. Kandace needed to get her car still, because we'd been too drunk to make the drive ourselves. As we were all seated, Austin tried to get the driver to drop him off at his hotel.

"No. I promised I'd look after you. You're not supposed to be alone," I said.

He shrugged. "I'll figure it out. Your room isn't big enough for both of us, and you need to lose the guilt."

Unlikely. "It was my fault, and I'm owning my mistake." The words came out with more of an edge than I intended. Apparently years of bitterness hadn't vanished because of a night of talking and a blowjob. I'd spent years giving myself reasons to resent him, and those hadn't magically disappeared.

Besides, it was my fault he was hurt.

"One of the partners at work owns property up ," Kandace said. "I can hook you both up for a few weeks. But I can't help with how this impacts your work."

Austin's scowl came out of nowhere.

"Are you all right?" Kandace asked. "Besides the obvious, I mean?"

"Yeah. I'll make it work. You both seem pretty set on this."

"Doctor's orders." I reminded him.

The driver looked in the rear view mirror at the three of us nestled in the back of his SUV. "Where to?" He asked again.

"Just the one spot." I gave him my address.

As he hit the freeway, Kandace sent a text to her

associate, and looked surprised when he called back almost immediately.

I was stunned too, given it was almost three in the morning.

"Didn't expect to hear back from you until tomorrow." She was cheerful as she answered. Even in the dark car, her blush at the reply was clear. "I didn't need to know that." Her laugh was embarrassed.

Hey, jealousy, welcome back. She was calling someone from work in the middle of the night, who replied immediately in a deep voice I could hear, even if I couldn't make out the words. He made her giggle, and she wasn't hesitating to borrow a house from him.

"I have a huge favor to ask," she said. "Let me rent your place off Main for a few months... Yeah, that one... He's not—" She glanced at me and the pink on her cheeks spread. "Okay, kind of, but it's not like that... yet.... I owe you, name your price." Another laugh. "Run that by Judith and let me know if you still feel the same... Uh-huh, I thought so. Thank you. See you Monday."

And with that, she hung up.

I was trying so hard not to be that guy. The one who expected someone I was involved with to not talk to anyone, ever.

"Good friend? Should we be jealous?" At least Austin cut straight to the point.

"Jealous... of Xander?" Kandace furrowed her brow. "Not unless you're hoping for a chance with his husband or their girlfriend. The three of them are very tight knit."

I was glad to hear it. But... husband and girlfriend? New thoughts were slinking into my head. Ridiculous thoughts because I still didn't like Austin and I barely knew Kandace. Though, I was getting to know more with each passing moment, and I liked pretty much all of it, my possessiveness aside.

When we reached Haddarville, Kandace redirected the driver to a different house, instead of the place I was staying. She had a code for the lockbox, and let us inside.

Austin picked a room on the main floor, and I claimed the one next to it, so I could hear him if he needed anything. I was too tired for a tour, but what I could see of the house, it was simple, clean, and nice.

And then I was alone with Kandace. "I had a lot of fun tonight," she said softly.

"It was a train wreck."

She smiled. "It was. I won't argue that for a second. And I never would have planned it or even agreed to it if I'd known up front. But it was still fun."

"Yeah, it was. And I'm not just saying that because of the blowjob and masturbation." Though... *wow*. I wrapped an arm around her waist. The gesture felt natural. Easy. "You're not driving home tonight. It's late."

"In that case, maybe we can address the one regret I have about the evening." She leaned her weight into me.

Fuck, that felt good. *She* felt good. Not just because my cock jerked at her closeness, but this was all so easy. "What's that?"

"That you and I didn't get to talk more."

I steered her toward the couch. "I don't know how long either of us will be awake, but no reason we can't start making up for that now, and pick up in the morning where we leave off."

She settled next to me on the cushions, and leaned into me when I wrapped an arm around her shoulder. She rested her head on my chest.

This was warm. Cuddly. Achingly sweet. And my ex-boyfriend-slash-de-facto-arch-nemesis was in the other room with a broken ankle, and regardless of what happened between Kandace and I, it was clear she was attracted to both of us.

This whole thing was a mess. But for tonight, I had her to myself.

I'd deal with reality later.

14
kandace

ELI and I moved into a bedroom before we completely passed out. I could've grabbed one of my own, but I was still riding the high of one of the most bizarre nights of my life, and for some reason sharing a bed when there were others in the house added to the madcap feeling.

Especially when I stripped down to a T-shirt and panties, and crawled under the blankets with Eli, who only wore boxer briefs. It was wicked and playful and made me feel like I was getting away with something naughty.

Because that was how devoid of excitement my life normally was.

Waking up the next morning to sunlight hitting my face was different. I was usually up long before this. What was that faint buzzing noise?

"Is that my phone?" When Eli mumbled the question, half-awake and still wrapped around me, the vibration teased over me. "Is it yours? Have the birds learned to use electric shavers?"

The ludicrous question, how easily it came to him, made me smile. "I'd love to know what the birds need to shave."

"Their nests. They use the things like little mini lawnmowers. Either that, or their balls."

My surprised laugh slipped out as I reached for my purse, where I'd left it on the nightstand. I swore I'd smiled and laughed more in the last twelve hours than in the last year. I grabbed my phone, to see if the noise was me.

I had five missed calls, and fifteen unread text messages. My gut sank as the device recognized my face and showed me previews of both. It looked like they were all from Lucas. I sat straight up, and scrolled through the texts first, because there were more and that was fastest.

"Everything all right?" Eli's tone shifted like that.

I held up a finger, to indicate I needed a minute. The first note was innocuous enough, and came in nearly three hours ago. *Hey, Mom. How was your date?*

From there, the messages slid to, *give me a call?*

Then *You're okay, right?*

I really need to talk.

Please call me back?

And became more insistent from there.

The voice mails were time-stamped after the text messages, though the content was about the same.

The last one ended with, "if you don't call me back in the next five minutes, I will freak the fuck out."

The actual freak-out had started about three hours ago, when I didn't answer his first couple of messages. I probably would've reacted the same way, and I was already dialing his number.

"Mom? Are you alive? Blink if you can't talk. Wait, I can't see you."

"I'm fine," I said before things could get worse. "I just overslept."

"Oh, God. Did they tie you up? Are they torturing you? Do you need ransom money? Give me your PIN. I promise to only drain as much cash as they want." Now he was teasing me.

"I promise, I'm fine." Though, it was a bit awkward having this conversation in front of Eli. I glanced over my shoulder to see him dressing quietly, and slipping from the room.

In my ear, Lucas sighed. "Okay. As long as you're all right." Something was off about his tone.

"Are you?" I asked.

Another sigh, this one heavier and more exaggerated. "I'm fine."

Uh-huh. Now that we'd moved past the *Mom's date unalived her* part of the conversation, I could find out why he'd messaged me to begin with. "What's wrong?"

"Mitch came over, and the studying was really good, and then I read the signals wrong, and oh. My. God. I tried to kiss him. My life is over."

I was never this kind of drama queen as a kid, but I was grateful Lucas felt comfortable expressing himself. If I'd done that with my own parents...

Anyway, "Are you sure that was what happened?"

"There aren't a lot of ways to interpret *mwah*"—he made a loud kissing sound—"*Oh, my phone, I need to go.*" His voice dropped an octave, I assumed to indicate that was what the other man had said.

"Unless he actually had to go." I suspected that things really had fallen apart, but I wouldn't jump to conclusions.

Lucas's sigh was pure frustration. "Sure. Will you be out all day with your date?" His tone softened.

I heard the underlying question. The one he wouldn't ask, but wanted to. *Will you be around to spend some time with me*? I wasn't going to leave him alone if he needed company. "I'm about an hour out. But as soon as I get back, I'll call you. We'll go get brunch."

"Thank you, Mom. Love you."

"Love you too." I hung up, and tugged on my clothes. While nothing about Lucas's situation was life-threatening or even dangerous, guilt settled in that I hadn't been available when he needed me. Worse, that I'd made him worry, especially on top of his freaking out.

With the sun dancing outside, and reality hovering around me, it was easy for me to put impulsive-Kandace back in her box. Sure, last night was a blast, the kind of thing I'd remember for ages, and probably tell Carly and Daria about, between wine and giggles.

Because I'd have to be a little tipsy to admit some of the things I'd done.

Masturbating to my one-night stand sucking off my maybe-boyfriend. Insane. And also, *H.O.T.*

Speaking of, I found both men in the kitchen, Joystick with his foot propped up on a second chair, and Eli sitting across from him. Neither was speaking.

I had no idea how they were going to make the next few weeks work, with the hot and cold they were already running.

"Everything all right?" Eli asked.

I nodded. "My son needs me. I have to go."

"I hope it's not bad." Joystick looked concerned.

"Nothing physical. His heart will recover, too." I didn't want to get into details, but I could give them enough to ease their worries.

Joystick's expression changed in a blink, and I was surprised a lightbulb didn't appear above his head. "You could bring him up here."

"I'd love to meet him," Eli added.

Yeah, no. That was exactly what I didn't need. *Hey, these are your childhood idols. They used to be in love, exactly like you thought, and by the way, one of them has his dick pierced and they give incredible orgasms. Ask me how I know.* "I think we're just going to hang out closer to home."

"Totally makes sense." Despite Joystick's words, his expression had fallen.

Eli wore a faint scowl as well.

I wanted to reassure him—them—but telling them they weren't my dirty little secret would be a lie. "But if you want me to grab any of your things while I'm down there, check you out of your hotel, I'd be happy to."

"That'd be great" Joystick's enthusiasm had gone. He gave me an address, his room key, and some information about what to grab.

So, uh… this was awkward. How did one say *see you later* after all of that?

"I'll walk you to the door." Eli to the rescue.

He and I paused on the front step. "I had a lot of fun last night." It was true, and it was something I should've said in front of Joystick, too.

"Me too. Can I see you again?"

"I'd like that." I also wanted to see Joystick again. Was that allowed? I also wanted to stay and hash things out. I also never wanted my son to know I was a deviant, or who I was doing things like that with.

Eli pressed his lips to my forehead. It was so sweet and intimate, and also strange coming from someone so much younger.

We said our goodbyes and I headed home. The worst thing about the long drive is it gave me so much time to overanalyze every single moment of the last twelve hours.

For work, being able to examine details from a removed perspective was critical. I had to be objective with my investments and decisions. It had always been the same in my personal life, and I was proud of that. So why weren't the answers coming now, and why did it feel like staying removed was a mistake?

Because I was letting my hormones do the thinking. A couple of gorgeous men gave me some attention and all the sudden I lost all sense of reason. Not good. Like with the night in Milan, there was no reason to cling to recent events as if they were some sort of bar for future decisions.

I could file away the memories and enjoy them, without having to do more reckless things. There. Problem sorted. Decision made. Time to move on

I repeated that over and over, because I needed to believe it. When I reached Salt Lake, I stopped at my house long enough to take a quick shower and change, then headed to Lucas's.

I knocked on his apartment door and waited. Seconds ticked away. For someone who had been so panicked a couple hours ago, he was taking a long time to answer. I was about to knock again, when I heard him saying, "Hang on. Just a sec."

The locks clicked, and he opened the door enough to stick his head into the crack. "Oh. Hey."

Mentally, I was raising my eyebrows at my perpetually-neat son's mussed hair, and the fact that his lips were puffy and red. "Hey."

"You made it."

"Do you still want to go get brunch?" I kept my tone kind and my expression neutral.

Lucas glanced behind him at something I couldn't

see, because the door wasn't open wide enough, then looked at me again. He raked his fingers through his hair. "Umm..."

"I can come back if you're busy." I wasn't blind. Apparently between *my social life is over* and now, he'd found someone to make out with.

"I'm sorry, I..." He managed to squeeze his body through the small opening, and step outside, so he could close the door behind him. His shirt was buttoned crooked, and his belt was missing. "Mitch came back," he whispered. "Last night his roommate needed him. But now..."

Right. Now the boys could pick up where they left off. The protective Mama Bear in me didn't like admitting my child was growing up this way, but I was rational. I was a reasonable human being. "Okay. Call me when you need me."

"Thank you." Lucas grinned, and vanished back into his apartment.

So much for that. As I walked back to my car, my stomach growled. I didn't want to go home, but I hated eating out alone. It always felt so awkward. Over the past six or so months, I'd become friends with a couple of the women at work—I hadn't really had girlfriends before, and I liked it. But Carly lived on the other side of the world with her boyfriends and their daughter, and Daria set weekends aside for time with her kids... and her boyfriends.

Which had me thinking about Eli and Joystick again. The biggest differences were that the two of them seemed to see everything as a competition, and I wasn't willing to be a prize. Though, in a way the idea was kind of sexy. But only in a fictional way, not in a real-life kind of way. And I wasn't the kind of woman who landed one guy, let alone two.

Fuck it, I'd go to breakfast alone.

The diner was packed, and no one cared who I was or that no one was with me. The food was good, the staff was fun, and I managed to silence my rambling thoughts for a short while.

As I was on my way out, I passed a group of women about half my age, laughing and waiting for a table. The one had violet and dark teal running through her mess of curls. I paused next to them. "Excuse me. I love your hair."

She grinned. "Yeah? I wasn't sure about the blue-green."

"It's perfect. A great contrast."

Her friends chimed in with enthusiastic agreements and *I told you so.*

"I wish I was brave enough for something like that." I didn't mean to say that out loud.

"Why wouldn't you be?" she asked.

I didn't have an answer. Pointing out I was older, and had things like business to worry about, felt rude. At least part of it would be a lie, too. Liz went through rainbow hair colors on a regular basis, and most of the other partners rarely batted an eye. The only answer I had was to shrug.

"If you find some courage…" the woman dug

through her purse, "…my friend did it for me, and she had a cancellation this afternoon. Give her a call and tell her Monique sent you."

"Thanks, I will." I wouldn't. I stuffed the card into my purse and walked back to my car.

Where I sat in the driver's seat, letting an onslaught of thoughts flood back in. How many times would I have to tell myself last night wasn't a repeatable thing, before the words sank in? How was everyone living life but me? I'd worked so hard, for so many years, and my reward was… to ignore what I wanted to do?

I pulled the hairdresser's card out again, and let the vibrant colors in her logo tease me.

Fuck it. Before I could question myself into oblivion, I let impulse dial the number. Thirty minutes later, I was in her chair, in a tiny salon. Four hours after that, I was staring at my reflection in her mirror, and didn't recognize the woman who stared back.

I'd opted for darker colors, and a combination of deep burgundy and rich purple framed my face.

"You look stunning, Hun." The hairdresser fluffed my hair again, and it fell in soft waves around my cheeks.

"I feel stunning. I feel like a different person."

"Nah. You're just a truer version of yourself."

I wasn't sure that was true, but I did love the way I looked. I paid, left her with a huge thanks and matching tip, and headed out. The day was almost over, and I hadn't done anything. How did I feel so good, in that case?

Next stop was Joystick's hotel room. Like in Milan, the place was simple and understated, but clean. It was easy enough to gather up his things, since it seemed he'd never unpacked. Really, the biggest disarray in the room was the paperwork spread across his desk.

It took me a moment to realize what I was looking at, and when I did my brain short-circuited. This wasn't at all what I expected from Joystick. I'd made some very incorrect assumptions about who he was.

15
joystick

I WAS surprised that Kandace didn't feel comfortable introducing us to her son, but I had a lot of respect for how close the two seemed to be. It was obvious she cared about him, and him her, after less than a day.

The hurt faded into oblivion when I popped the next round of drugs for the pain, and I fell into sleep quickly after breakfast. Years ago, when I hit adulthood and the public started getting wind of my tattoos and piercings, everyone assumed I'd gone full party boy.

I'd tried it a few times, to see what all the fuss was about, but it wasn't my thing. Nights like last night were as drunk as I got, and things like prescription pills knocked me on my ass like any lightweight.

When Kandace stopped by with my stuff, I was still in that happy haze. Something was different about her. *Oh.* "You turned into a purple-haired angel-raven."

Her smile was its own drug, especially the flush that came with it. "I'm not sure I know what that is, but thanks?"

"If you need a messenger, beautiful angel-raven, call on me." I kissed the back of her hand, and ignored Eli rolling his eyes.

The rest of the weekend, I fluctuated between groggy and aching, with a few pauses for food. The hospital called Sunday afternoon and said they'd fit me in for surgery the next morning. I hoped it wasn't just because the doctor's kid was a fan. I'd feel bad if I jumped the schedule line.

I also felt bad that Eli took Monday off work, to make sure I got to the hospital, and home again. By the time we got back to the house, from surgery, I was tired of feeling like a foggy-headed mess, and I decided to skip the meds for a few hours.

Large cotton candy clouds still lingered in my head, but I could see the light of brain-workingness through them. A pair of crutches leaned next to my bed. I'd used them to get in here, but it was with Eli's help. Otherwise, it had been a few decades since I had a need for something like that.

Still, how hard could it be to relearn?

I scooted myself to the edge of the bed. My bags sat in the corner—I'd have to go through those later, and also make sure I gave Kandace a real thank you for bringing them to me.

Pulling the crutches to me, I fumbled a few times before I figured out how to stand upright with them in place. The concept was simple, but the execution took some maneuvering. As I hopped/swung/limped my way across the bedroom, trying to get used to two aluminum legs and one good one, I thumped enough to shake the floor.

By the time I reached the doorway, Eli was there. "Are you all right?" He asked.

"I won't win any three legged races any time soon." Wait. What? "Was that funny? Did it even make sense?" I might not be as clear-headed as I thought.

"Are you sure you should be up?"

"I spent more than two days in bed. I'm sure I'm tired of lying around doing nothing."

Eli's back and forth motion made it seem like he wasn't sure if he should move closer or further away. "Do you want help?"

"I think I need to figure this out on my own. If I remember correctly, the living room is only a few kilometers away."

Eli furrowed his brow. "Kilometers? I have so many ques— Are you joking or still high?"

"I have no idea." It wasn't really funny, so probably the latter.

The way Eli lingered nearby while I pushed myself into the living room was both sweet and unnerving. I settled into a recliner that looked like it hadn't been used in a while, so he probably hadn't claimed it. I could lean back, but I'd spent the last few days lying down.

Eli nudged an ottoman in my direction, and I lifted my cast-covered leg onto it with a grateful smile. He grabbed a set of keys off the table and shoved them in his pocket, but not before I caught a glimpse of *Nevada* keychain with an *E* on it. The one I'd bought for him when we first ran into each other again.

That warmed my heart.

This was the first time I'd gotten a good look at the house beyond my room. The living room was furnished with plenty of seating for company, and while it was all clean, it also looked like a place where people gathered and enjoyed themselves, rather than it being sterile and stiff.

My gaze landed on a familiar object in the corner, near the kitchen doorway. "Is that my guitar?"

"Kandace brought everything she found in your room. I didn't realize you still played."

"I don't. Rather, I don't play well." I'd never gotten the hang of it. "Not like you do. But I can pluck out the chords. It's a fun trick to use when I want to get laid."

Eli rolled his eyes.

Was that a step up from scowling? "*You* still play though."

"I don't do command performances." Despite the words, Eli was focused on the acoustic guitar.

When we were kids, we had one episode with a guitar, and Eli only needed to learn enough to look convincing during filming. He'd picked the instrument up, though. Back then it seemed to come naturally to him, and I hoped he'd stayed in practice. "What if I ask nicely instead of commanding?"

"That's not—" Eli sighed.

"Listen—I'm not lucid enough to do work, and I'm tired of sleeping. Do you want to talk about the past? Watch TV?" I didn't suspect he wanted to do either of those things, and maybe I should drop the topic, but I remembered how good he was, and at least back then, no one knew he'd kept playing besides me. It felt like *our thing*.

And I was still trying to find any angle I could to get Eli's friendship back. More would be better, especially if Kandace was part of that, but I could start with friendship.

Eli looked like he was going to argue some more, but instead he crossed the room to grab the guitar. He plucked out a couple of chords and winced. "This is so out of tune."

"Oops?" I shrugged, not apologetic at all.

He spent the next few minutes tuning the device by ear, and it was simple but delightful. Eli became so beautifully focused so quickly.

He let out a huff that I assumed meant *let's do this*, perched on the edge of the couch, and strummed out a few notes. "What do you want to hear?"

More of what I'd just caught a hint of. A song we both loved back then. "What's your default? I don't have any idea what you know."

"Then I have the perfect thing." The tone of the

song changed instantly. I wasn't sure what this was until he started singing, too. About doing just fine before he met me. Drinking. Hoping to not see my friends again. It was Closer by The Chainsmokers.

And the lyrics hit like a fist around my heart.

Eli kept his gaze on his fingers, never looking at me.

"My mistake for making you choose. How about Linkin Park's In Between?" I sang the first few lines about apologizing. Getting caught in between.

"We're not doing this." Eli talked over me.

Passive aggressively arguing via music? "You started it." Way to be an adult, me. But I had a better idea, and I wanted to make this work. I grabbed a tin off the table next to me, and it rattled like it had pins inside it. Inspiration struck, and I shook out an almost-tambourine-like beat. The opening rhythm to Do You Wanna Be My Girl by Jet.

Eli raised an eyebrow, but he came in on guitar at the right time. The music and lyrics hit differently in acoustic form, but the longer he sang, the more his expression lightened. The entire song made me think of both him and Kandace, and the upbeat music was fast and fun.

We moved from one pop-beat to another. It seemed like most of what he knew was either about heartbreak or love, but a lot of songs were, so that made sense.

When I heard the familiar notes of Follow You Down by Gin Blossoms again, the ache in my chest was back. I tried to keep my tone light as we sang the opening verse together. We reached the chorus, and I was still singing when I realized the music had stopped.

Eli moved the guitar to rest on the ground. "I'm done. Do you need help getting to bed?"

The instant shift in mood was horrible. "No. I might sit up a little longer."

Eli stood, returned the guitar to its spot, and walked from the room.

No, this wasn't ending this way. I scrambled to my feet as fast as possible, grabbed my crutches, and hobbled after him. I reached Eli's room as he was letting the door swing shut, and I stuck one crutch in the way.

"Why did you follow me? Your foot…" Eli opened the door again. "You're an idiot."

I met his gaze. "No. I'd be an idiot to let you leave on a note like that one."

"What do you want from me, Austin?"

Everything. But it was too soon for that. "A second chance at friendship."

"You're here. I'm here."

"Because you blame yourself for this." I nodded at my cast.

Eli raked his fingers through his hair. "I don't hate you, but I've spent the last fifteen years thinking I should. That doesn't go away overnight, but I'm trying to let it go."

It was a good starting point. "I'll take it."

16
elijah

WAS I willing to admit to myself that the living room sing-in with Austin was fun?

Yes. The memories hurt, but not all of them. I'd been honest with him before I disappeared into my room—I was currently torn between years of pent-up loathing, and realizing my fond memories of the past weren't all tainted by nostalgia.

Austin had been, and still was, an okay guy.

A guy that once upon a time, I'd thought I was falling in love with.

Over the years I'd convinced myself anything I felt for him back then was because I was dumb and naive and didn't know any better. The last couple of days were making me question more than a decade of resentment.

On top of that, I still felt bad that Austin was stuck here, hurt and down and out for at least a few months. That was definitely my fault.

Letting my mind race in a loop all night wouldn't do me any good. I wanted to focus instead on work. What a great opportunity this movie was.

And on Kandace. I wanted to talk to Kandace.

I sent her a quick text. *How was your day?*

Good. Her answer came through quickly.

And now she was in my head full-force. When she showed up with Austin's things the other day, she'd looked incredible, and he was frustratingly adorable, hopped up on painkillers, telling her she looked like an angel-raven, and making her blush.

How's it going there? Her next text buzzed me back to the conversation. *How's Joystick?*

And there was my trickle of envy that she'd asked me about him. Though, I might have done the same. *He's good. I'm good.*

Good.

This wasn't working for me. It was too stilted. What would Austin do?

It didn't matter, because I was me, and I knew what I wanted to do. I dialed her number.

"Hello?" She almost sounded surprised when she answered.

"Hey. I wanted to hear your voice."

"Oh." Her blush was almost audible in that one sound. "I'm glad."

"I'm not interrupting, am I?"

"No. I was going to watch The Bachelorette, but this is better."

I was about to be *that guy* who ruined the fun. "You realize that show is all but scripted, don't you?"

"I assumed it wasn't completely improv or real. Even if all they do is shove these people into very specific situations, it's easy enough to guess they'll react in certain ways."

They ought to put cameras in the house here, with Austin and me. They'd get one hell of a show. *Odd Couple, the Millennial Edition.*

My insides twisted and recoiled at the notion. It was bad enough having hints of my romance with him on display the first time around.

Romance? This wasn't romance.

I needed to be talking to Kandace. "You ever feel bad for any of them?" I asked.

"Yes and no? The first couple of seasons, when it was a new thing and no one really knew what to expect? More so. Now people should have a good idea of what they're getting themselves into. You know what I do dislike though? That she has to pick one at the end."

I wasn't looking forward to that either. "She's not going to be compatible with all twelve or thirteen of them."

"True."

I didn't want to talk about picking and choosing between men, for that way madness lay. Or at least a lot of jealousy that I wasn't in the mood to confront. "What else do you like to watch? To read?"

"Really dry, dull stuff."

"No, really. It can't be that bad."

"I'm a tech investor. I spent a lot of time reading up on where people are spending, what they're inventing, and trending the two toward each other for future projections." The way she said it, it was almost sexy.

Or I was biased and just liked hearing when she said anything. I lay back on my bed, to get comfortable. It was so easy to imagine her here next to me. Cuddling after a long day. Talking. "There's got to be some interesting stuff in there. Future tech means robots that can be Bachelorette contestants, right?"

Kandace laughed. "Probably. I suspect they're better in bed."

"You mean specifically, not overall, right?" Because if I thought I had to prove I was better than Austin, there was no fucking way an imaginary sex robot was going to get top billing over me.

"If you can program them..." Kandace trailed off.

"Then they're following a script again. Say you're in the mood one night, and you pick *slow seduction* from the menu. You get a few minutes into it and you realize you want *hard, rough, and dirty* instead. A real person can adapt." Was I really doing this?

Apparently so.

Kandace made a clucking sound with her tongue. "Not all real people can adapt, and can I stash a real person in the cupboard at the end of the night?"

"If that's their kink? Probably. You don't want that though."

"No? What do I want?"

"Stimulation." I was about to get myself in trouble. It was rare that people actually wanted to hear what I'd observed, even if I thought it was good.

The light huff Kandace let out was hard to interpret. "Yes, that's what we're talking about."

"Not just physical, but mental too."

"Go on."

"You're not a person who settles." And here I went anyway. I was going to misstep, she was going to get offended, and the conversation would be over. But I'd started, and stopping now wouldn't be any better. "You need someone who can keep up with you in a conversation, and since we're talking about sex, you'd prefer if they could get you off, too. Someone like me."

"You want to apply for the job of... live-in-robot-vibrator?" Her question was playful.

"No. I'm applying for the job of boyfriend."

"Well, there's not a line of twelve other men behind you, but you do still need to prove your qualifications." Her tone was professional but fun. "Tell me why you're the man for the job."

"I know a lot of random stories about a lot of random celebrities."

She sighed. "So does my brother."

Definitely didn't want to go down the path of comparing me to someone she was related to. "I'm a great conversationalist."

"True. But so are my colleagues."

Ouch. She was actually going to make me earn this.

That was fair, and it should be a fun challenge. What now? "I've been fantasizing since I met you about all the things I'd like to do to you when I finally get you alone. These aren't generic fuck fantasies. They're exclusive to, and have only ever starred you."

"Really." Was that a catch in her voice? "I'm going to need details. Tell me about a time you fantasized about me." Her voice was definitely breathier than before.

"The other day, between the trailers, I was giving some serious consideration to the best way to make you come."

"Out in public?" Kandace sounded intrigued rather than bothered.

My cock twitched with the memories and the expectation of where this conversation was heading. "There was no one around."

"Someone found us."

I was grateful she didn't say his name, but if I'd done what I'd wanted to next, and Austin discovered us... "With a little luck they'd want to watch."

"Is that the fantasy? Being watched?"

That was at least a dozen unique fantasies, all starring Kandace and me, and most with Austin in the audience. "It's one of them. Taking you in front of other people. Stripping you down. Slipping my fingers inside you. You'd be so wet. So turned on by the attention, knowing that everyone was watching us. Wanting to be me, because only I could touch you. Only I could taste your pussy. Only I could finger and fuck you until you screamed with pleasure. Until you couldn't walk and couldn't think and could only collapse in my arms when you were satisfied."

And now I was hard as a rock. I stroked my good hand over my cock, through my jeans, but the pressure only made me want more.

Especially combined with Kandace's heavier breathing, echoing in my ear. "Wow." Her voice was so soft. So seductive. "And that's just one fantasy?"

"I have a vivid imagination." One that was currently trying to process too many images at once. I wanted to hear her come. I wanted to get her off *now*. "I'm so hard thinking about this. I wish I was there, so we could actually live one of these."

"As much as I like that first one, I don't see it happening on a next date. So tell me what we'd actually do if we were in the same room." Everything she said was a tease, though she probably didn't intend it that way.

I could tease too. "Not sure I want to tell you."

"Why not?" Her pout was practically audible.

"Not unless I know it's turning you on."

"I promise you it is."

"Show me."

Silence met me. Was the conversation over? My phone buzzed and I pulled it away from my ear to read the text.

Which contained a stunning close-up view of

Kandace's bare breasts, including the little heart on the left one. The text itself said *earn the next one.*

I grinned. Reasonable request. "If I was with you right now, I'd take my time. Exploring every inch of your breasts. Playing with those big, pink nipples until they were swollen and puffy. Pinching. Biting. Making you squirm. Fuck, I can't do this."

"Do what?" Kandace's disappointment was nearly tangible.

"I'm taking out my cock. I can't keep it locked away during this."

"Show me." The way she turned my own words back on me, the challenge in her voice as I wrapped my hand around my shaft, made my entire body shudder.

I liked this so fucking much. I'd never sent a dick pic in my life—talk about tacky—but tonight... I fisted my cock, clicked a picture, and hit *Send.*

"I'd have so much fun wrapping my lips around you," Kandace said a moment later.

A fresh memory flashed in my mind, of how Austin felt, kneeling at my feet, *apologizing.* Was this a mistake? No. Because I liked the memory, and Kandace was in my head too.

Though, I *only* wanted to think about her. "You come first." I gripped my shaft loosely, but didn't stroke. My light touches combined with the images of her hand replacing mine, were enough teasing for now. "When you're begging for more, I'd lick down your body. Since this is fantasy, we're already naked."

"Good. Clothes get in the way."

"I'd bury my tongue inside you and let you ride my face. You taste incredible, and I'd dine down there for so long, fingering your clit until you came on my tongue again and again." I tried to keep from stroking myself too fast.

But the way Kandace's breathing came in short pants had me aching for more.

"Are you touching yourself?" I asked.

"Yes, but it's not the same as having you do it."

My phone buzzed again, and this time she was sending me video of her fingers buried in her slick, wet pussy. I could hear every gasp, and combined with the visual…

"God, I can't forget how good you taste," I groaned out the words. "Make yourself come for me. I need to hear it."

Kandace's gasps grew louder, and I stroked myself harder as she fingered her swollen clit. The angle of the camera was wrong. The lighting was wrong. I didn't care. Seeing her clench as she got closer—

The camera angle changed abruptly, and I was looking at a ceiling. It didn't matter. I could still hear Kandace gasping. Whimpering. Crying out when she climaxed.

The noises, the teasing built, it all came together and I came too, covering my hand and halfway up my stomach. I was grunting, and only barely aware that I wasn't alone in the house and shouldn't get too loud.

For a moment only silence and the sounds of our breathing filled the room. And then Kandace's giggle came through the phone.

"If I was there right now, I'd be kissing you so hard." If I couldn't cuddle, at least I could offer this. "Letting you taste yourself on my lips. On my fingers. Lick your fingers for me."

"No." Her answer caught me off-guard.

"Why not?"

"Not until you're actually here."

Fuck me. How was this so intensely incredible? "Then next time we do this, it's in person. Next time, you're not giving yourself any orgasms. That's my job."

Her laugh was back. "If you insist."

"I do. I want to see you Friday night."

"That's so far away. Waiting will be so hard." She exaggerated half the words.

I was about to find out just how hard. It would be worth it, though. "Think of me until then. No touching yourself, though."

"Really?"

"Really," I said. "Your next orgasm is mine."

"My next orgasm is yours," Kandace agreed. "Good night, Eli."

"Good night, Kandace." I didn't want to hang up, but I made myself do so.

The warm fuzzy feeling lingered through the night, and was there the next morning when I got ready for work. I was hard in the shower, thinking about the conversation with Kandace.

On my way out the door, I paused to say *goodbye* to Austin, but he was still hidden in his room. Instead, I made sure the cereal was easy for him to reach, so he could have breakfast.

The short drive to the filming location gave me more time to think about Kandace. I was so completely smitten. I wasn't sure if it was my mood that helped the morning go so well, or if it was just a good day.

A little before lunch, Andrew tracked me down. He had a woman by his side who had long, dark hair, and was about my age. She was objectively attractive, but I had someone else on my mind.

"This is Isabella." Andrew introduced her. "We've just cast her in Tara's role."

We'd had a hard time filling that part. Andrew wanted someone who was actually Italian, who spoke the language, and we'd found the perfect actress, but she'd gotten a higher paying offer somewhere else.

If Andrew liked her, that was fine with me. I shook her hand. "Pleasure to meet you."

17
kandace

PHONE SEX.

First masturbating while two people got each other off, and then phone sex.

Who was I?

When did Eli and Joystick's roles in my life trade places? Eli was the one I was having the filthy fantasies about, and I wanted to spend time seeing what was going on in Joystick's brain.

But saying they'd traded places wasn't a fair way to put it. I'd spent just enough time with each of them to admit neither was a two-dimensional outlet for my years of pent-up frustration. Neither was a fling or a wild way for me to forget for a few hours at a time that I was a responsible adult.

That presented a new problem because wild-Kandace and boring-normal-plain-Kandace both wanted both men. What was I supposed to do with that?

The conundrum taunted me for days, mingling with me thinking about Joystick's restaurant plans of all things. If he were anyone else, if he came to me with an idea like the one I'd seen spread out on his desk, I'd want to help him grow it.

It wasn't the kind of project I invested in. Raul and Diego were as much diversification for me as anything, and their chain would hit a wider audience. But what Joystick was doing... It was still unique. Fascinating. The kind of thing I'd love to be involved in.

The thing was, he hadn't come to me. He hadn't asked me for help. Offering felt like overstepping.

And I wanted to go out with him again. Without having to give up Eli.

Thursday morning, I wrapped up a small team call, and Carly stayed on the phone to chat. It was a shame I hadn't realized I could be friends with her until right before she moved to Italy.

I was glad she'd taken the job to manage our European office, though—she was top notch at the job. And I was happy for her and the love she'd found.

"Did Joystick ever find you?" Her question came out of left field.

"What?"

"I know, I'm a horrible friend. I should've told you the minute he left here, and I meant to, but it's not the kind of thing one drops in a text, and we haven't had a chance to talk until now."

No. Really. "What?"

"Are you going deaf in your old age?" She teased.

Smart ass. I wasn't even five years older than she was. "I've seen him. He wasn't looking for me."

"I assure you, he was." Most of the time when Carly spoke, it was with confidence, and this didn't seem like the kind of thing she would joke about.

I'd known Joystick was spending a lot of time with Diego and Raul in Italy. Supposedly he clicked with them immediately when he met them. After the time I'd spent with Joystick, it was easy to believe he made most of his friends by sheer force of will and existence.

Curiosity won out and I had to know, "why do you think he was looking for me?"

"Because of the way he talked about you while he was here. Nothing big. Nothing overt. Little questions here and there. Have you noticed he's not exactly a subtle guy?"

"I have."

"Except when it came to trying to find out about you," Carly said.

Oh. But why me? "The whole thing with him is complicated."

"Is it? Or do you just not want to explain?"

Given the way I was struggling to wrap my brain around the whole thing, I was pretty sure it was complicated. "Fine. you know how my brother is finally making his movie."

"Not sure you mentioned that," Carly teased.

Fair point. I was proud of what Andrew was doing, and I'd bragged a little. "So I'm dating the fixer he hired for his screenplay."

"Since when?"

Was dating even the right word? After last night I was pretty sure. "Since... not long?"

"And Joystick found out and he's insanely jealous."

"Not quite." I sucked my teeth. "The writer, Elijah—"

"Was Joystick's co-star on Donovan. Fuck me." Carly filled in several blanks for me.

I shrugged, though she couldn't see me. How did she know that?

"Like I said, he talked a lot when he was here. Told a lot of stories," Carly answered my unspoken question.

Right, then. "So you understand, Joystick came to the movie lot to find Eli, not me."

Carly let out a long breath. "That does almost qualify as complicated. You win. But you're banging them both." She said it like a fact, not a question. "Same time or separately?"

"It's not like that."

"Do you want it to be?"

"Maybe." Definitely. I couldn't see them getting along well enough for that in the near future. Though that blowjob they shared...

I mentally cleared my throat.

"What's stopping you? Go for it, woman," Carly

said.

"I don't know." But I did know, it just felt improper to admit it.

Carly was in love with two men, who very much loved each other. So were Daria and Brooke, who I hung out with on those rare occasions when our schedules lined up.

Why did I think being with two men wasn't proper? "It's complicated."

"Uh-huh. Hang on." There was muffled talking on Carly's side for a minute. "Ellie wants me to read her the bedtime story she wrote. I'll call you back. We'll figure this out."

"It's late there. Go to bed. I've got this." I wasn't going to keep Carly up all night with my inability to make a decision.

"Okay. But remember, regardless of what Joystick said, he's there to see you."

"He's not. 'Night, Carly."

I hung up, but that didn't erase the conversation from my thoughts. Joystick came here looking for me. I wasn't the only one that night had an impact on. He'd been asking about me. Acting differently because of *me*.

Why? I was just me. He was a sexy, outgoing, famous guy who could have anyone he wanted.

Almost.

My phone chimed with a new text from Carly. It was a phone number and said *call him*.

I couldn't help but smile at the less than subtle

nudge. If what she said was true—and she tended to be bluntly honest—that made me feel less awkward about reaching out to Joystick.

I summoned the courage of whatever wicked spirit prompted me to send Eli dirty pictures the other night, and dialed Joystick's number. When he answered, we made the most basic of small talk. How was my work? How was his foot?

This wasn't what I wanted. "I saw your restaurant plans," I said.

"Yeah? What did you think?"

"I love what you're doing." Geek themed dining. Store with merch in one half of the building, and a restaurant in the other. Not completely unique, but the way he had it set up stood out.

"Because it's epic, right?" Joystick asked.

Without question. "You've got an incredible plan."

"But you have notes." He zeroed in on my reasons for bringing it up.

I did, but I hoped he'd see them as the kind of good that I did. "Tweaks. Suggestions. There's nothing wrong with your idea, but there are alternatives to consider. Like when you're painting a room and white or off white could both be the right answer, but you want to make sure you consider each equally."

Joystick let out a short laugh. "I don't know if I've ever willingly painted a room any shade of white."

Of course he hadn't. Horrible example.

"I want to hear all your thoughts, though," he

said. "To be honest, I was trying to keep this a secret until it was in the right shape to show you, but now that you've seen it..."

"I can come up and visit. We could talk it out." The offer came easily, before I could consider how he might interpret it. This was work talk. This was what I did. It was simple to slide into owning it.

"Friday afternoon? Carly tells me the office frequently takes half of tomorrow off."

He really had been asking about me. Would it be weird for me to see Joystick right before Eli?

Of course not, because this was business.

Yeah, I didn't believe that for a second. Still, I wasn't hiding what was going on from either of them...

This really was complicated. "Friday sounds good, but I can't stay too late, I have a date."

Silence greeted me.

I was grasping for a follow-up comment, when Joystick said, "Stunning woman like you? Of course you do. Don't suppose he lives in the same house as me?"

"He does right now, yes."

"Then I can keep you until he picks you up, and maybe pick your brain again the next morning."

I swore there was a hint of something less-than-cheerful in Joystick's reply. Was this about to be a bad idea or a really good one?

Only way to find out was to go ahead with the whole thing.

18
joystick

Was I like a kid on Christmas Eve, every time I thought about seeing Kandace again?

More than it was probably smart to admit.

I was owning the desire anyway.

Not only was she stopping by this afternoon, but things had been mostly antagonism-free with Eli for the last few days. Not super friendly, not yet, but I'd take quiet Eli over stand-offish Eli every single day of every single month.

Though, the Eli I'd prefer was the one I overheard the other night when he was talking to Kandace. The walls here weren't paper thin of anything, and I was doing my best not to listen in. But my room was right next to his, and what had started as little snippets of conversation drifting my way became some blatant grunting, and what sounded like an intense orgasm.

That was the Eli I wanted—phone sex and fun Eli.

But for now, I was in the living room waiting for

Kandace. It hadn't taken me long to get used to the crutches, but that didn't mean I was supposed to be zipping around everywhere. The only thing making me obey the doctor's orders was that I didn't want to be trapped in this cast longer than I had to be.

Fortunately, the place was nice and the company wasn't bad either.

At the sound of a knock, I called, "Come in." The door opened. "Unless you're here to do wicked things to me," I added.

"I might be." Kandace stepped into the room. "What's your opinion on the sexiness of five year profit-loss projections?" She looked better than I remembered. Every time I saw her.

And the hair really did make her look like an angel-raven. My pill induced haze got that detail right. "Sounds kinda hot the way you say it. The bad news, I've already done mine," I teased. "But I'm always happy to let you take a peek under the hood."

"Oh good." Kandace hung her coat by the front door and moved closer into the room. "I like to watch."

This was still the Kandace I met in Italy—smart, funny, and stunning. But she was a few notches more bold, and I liked it.

"I was hoping you'd participate." I patted the seat next to me. "Maybe in some property evaluations?"

She sucked in a sharp breath and caught her bottom lip between her teeth. *"Hot."* The weight of her hip against mine when she sat was definitely that—*Hot*.

"Can I get you a drink? How was your drive up?" I all but stumbled over the words. Was I nervous?

A little. This wasn't just flirting. It wasn't seduction at all. I was moving out of my comfort zone and into Kandace's world, and it was clear from the way she and Eli clicked that she liked her men smart. Not that I was the village idiot, but I knew what most people wanted me for and it wasn't my intelligence.

"I'm good," Kandace said. "The drive was good."

"Then we should get started, so I can glean as much of your expertise as possible in the time we have." It might be more fun to flirt and play all afternoon, but this was a project that actually mattered to me, and I truly wanted her for her knowledge.

Kandace pulled out her laptop, and when she opened it, a series of diagrams and notes overlapped on the small screen. She'd thought about this a lot.

"How long did you spend looking at my notes?" I was in awe at what she was flipping through.

Kandace shrugged. "I gave them a glance as I put them away. It felt rude to sit and read them all without your permission, but I couldn't help a peek." She sounded apologetic.

"You can examine my notes anytime, for as much time as you want."

The flush on her cheeks was one of those things I'd come to adore about her.

She dove into her ideas. Some of her suggestions

were things I'd thought of, and some were unique. Ideas I never would've considered. She was right, this was the kind of thing that gave a project polish.

It was brilliant.

Even better was how into the whole thing she was. Her enthusiasm seemed genuine, for this idea that had grabbed me a few months ago and refused to let go.

I'd been adrift for a long time, since dialing back the acting jobs. I hated to admit it even in my own head, but I wanted more than being *Donovan*, and getting jobs because nostalgia called for it. My fans were the best, and I wasn't planning on stepping out of the spotlight, but this idea was mine. A business concept that reflected me, and let me share that appreciation with the world.

"You mentioned location," Kandace said. "Where are you thinking of opening up?"

"Demographically? Utah. There's a huge geek population here, and while it's a tough market to crack, I think I have the right concept."

"More specifically, what cities are you considering? Where are you looking at property?"

Nowhere. "I scouted several locations online. Lehi, Herriman, Sandy, Layton..." All part of the different metropolitan areas out here, from what I'd seen. "Every viewing appointment I had was canceled when the rumors hit that I was building something vile."

"How did those get out?" Kandace typed something else, her fingers flying across the keyboard.

Not a fucking clue. "Still trying to figure that out, but I've been working on smoothing things over with the fans. They know me. They know it's not true."

"Good. You should focus on that." She grabbed her phone. "I have the perfect solution for everyone else." She stood as she dialed.

This wasn't the shy woman I'd gotten locked in the park with so many months ago. This Kandace was direct. Confident. Knew exactly what she was doing, what she wanted, and how to get it done.

So. Fucking. Sexy.

I listened to her half of a conversation that was basically a repeat of what she and I had just discussed, and that ended with her, "Great, I'll let him know. You're the best, thank you."

Kandace disconnected. "That was Lyndsay, our social media manager—and she is the best at positive PR. She's the one who smoothed things over when the fake wedding news broke about Carly, Raul, and Diego."

"Okay?" I'd heard good things about that.

"Her son is traveling this weekend for a wrestling match, and she was trying to figure out how to spend her time." Kandace settled next to me again. "She'll be here tomorrow to help you map out a plan."

That was kind of both of them, but, "I handle my own social media. I'm sure your person is great, but I talk to my own fans."

"I know. I've seen, and they love you for it. She's not going to take over your accounts. She's for damage control outside of your fan base, and she'll make a few suggestions for you going forward, that's all optional."

I wouldn't be taking the suggestions, regardless of who they came from, but I did like the idea of someone dealing with the doubters who didn't follow me. "I'm not asking her to work for free. What's her fee?"

"I have it covered."

No. Free consultation from Kandace was a blurry line, but if she started bringing in more people from her office... "You're absolutely not the one paying her if she's working for me."

Kandace pursed her lips and looked like she was ready to argue. "I'll have her invoice you."

"Thank you."

"So... I have a list of vendors who might be useful to you." Kandace's tone had shifted. It wasn't obvious, but the ease had faded and was replaced with formality. "You may already have several of these, but just in case."

This wasn't just because I'd insisted on paying people who worked for me, was it? Couldn't be. Regardless, I wanted the fun back. "Why do you like this idea?" I asked.

"Because it's a great idea."

"Of course it is. But you strike me as the kind of

person who wants to be passionate about a project. Why this one?"

Kandace clasped and unclasped her hands, and turned to meet my gaze. "Because *you're* passionate about it. It's clear you love the idea, and you want to bring it to other people who love the same things. But it's more than that. You've put a solid plan in place for execution. It's not just *ooh, this sounds fun*, but you've figured out how to make it happen. The world would be a better place if more people could follow their dreams."

She spoke with so much sincerity, with such depth and warmth, that I didn't know how to reply. Instinct said *make this light*. My brain wanted to come back with *You're in my dreams nightly. Help me follow those?*

"You got all of that from a glance?" I said.

One corner of her mouth tugged up. "You sold me with your elevator pitch, and that says a lot. Knowing the person behind the project doesn't hurt either—if anyone can pull this off, you can."

Oh. I'd been a lot of things for a lot of people, and that almost always involved what they needed my name or face for. Did she really like me for my brain?

We spent the next couple of hours planning and flirting. It was a great combination.

I couldn't help my disappointment when the front door latched open, and Eli walked in. As his scowl flashed into place then vanished behind a smile that didn't reach his eyes, the pit in my chest grew heavier.

19
elijah

I KNEW I'd see Austin and Kandace together when I got back to the house, but the sight still filled me with intense ambivalence. Was I jealous that they looked like they were having fun? I should be, but mostly I wanted to be a part of it.

The instant Austin saw me, he gathered up the stack of papers he was holding and shoved them back in their folder. "Look. Your date's here. Time to go." His tone was light and not forced.

Then again, his tone was rarely forced. He'd always been easy-going.

"Are you sure you don't have any more questions?" Kandace was more methodical about making a few clicks on her computer, typing a few things, before closing the laptop.

Austin shook his head. "Nothing that won't wait until tomorrow."

Because his assumption was that tomorrow she'd still be here. I liked that thought.

"Okay. You crazy kids should be on your way." Austin made a shooing motion toward the door.

I wasn't sure what to make of the behavior. "That eager to get rid of us?"

"Nope. But I crashed your date last time, so you should go have a real one tonight. Just the two of you," Austin said.

It won't be the same without you there. The unexpected response bubbled up in my throat, and I swallowed it. I looked at Kandace. "Give me a few minutes to change and such, and we'll go?"

"Sounds great," she said.

I felt like a giddy kid again, for the second time in as many Fridays. I'd already gotten to spend a lot of time with Kandace, and the phone conversation the other night still teased my dreams, but *first date* had a sweet-but-high-pressure ring to it. So I tried to force a balance between freshening up and hurrying as fast as was physically fucking possible, and a few minutes later I found her in the living room, exactly where I'd left her next to Joystick.

"Shall we be off?" I offered a hand, she accepted, and I tugged her to her feet.

We said our goodbyes to Austin, who promised not to wait up, with a series of less than subtle winks, and Kandace and I headed out.

The sun had already gone down, though it was

barely six, but the air was still warm. Early spring would be nice. "I was thinking," I said as we walked side by side toward the street. "I keep seeing this little town, every day, and I haven't really explored it yet." Just like I hadn't gotten to explore Kandace yet. "And I want to get to know you better. Walking seems like a great way to do both, if you're up for it." I offered my arm.

She hooked her hand around my elbow. "Sounds lovely. I'm in."

The house was only a block from the end of Main Street, so we headed in that direction. It felt natural to be this close to her. Warm. Inviting. Enticing.

Too bad I couldn't think of a single thing to say. I'd spent the day touching up witty dialogue for Andrew's film, and when it came to my own conversations? The best I had was *nice weather, eh?*

Nope. I wasn't going to be a small-talk guy. Not like that.

We rounded the corner to the town's main thoroughfare. The sidewalks were busier than the rest of the week, but that still wasn't the kind of packed I was used to in bigger towns. I liked it. A handful of the buildings were boarded up and shuttered, but a lot more of them were open. Most still with the classic facings, but well-maintained.

"The hardware store has been in the family forever." Kandace nodded at one building across the street from us. "Inside you'll find the normal hardware stuff —hammers, saws, nails, gardening supplies. And then on the other half of the store, it almost looks like you stepped into a Radio Shack or a mad scientist's lab. Evie insists capacitors and circuit boards have as much right to exist in a hardware store as self-tapping screws."

"I can't argue with logic like that."

Kandace jerked a thumb toward the building we were next to. It had a more subtle look, and no sign on the awning. But the door proclaimed it was a new age tea shop. "If crystals are your thing, Sebastian's got them. He insists he doesn't believe, and that he only keeps the stock to honor his grandmother, but his regular clients say he's got a gift for knowing what they need to cleanse their auras on any given day. He also has more flavors of tea than I've ever seen in a single place."

"That's pretty cool." Only two shops in, and this place was already quirkier and more fun than something straight out of an eighty's movie.

As we continued our journey down the street, Kandace had a story about almost every business we passed. The vintage clothing store, the coffee shop, and the antique store. "He found a secret basement full of sex furniture a year or so ago," she said about Deacon's. "And the record store—"

"Wait." I couldn't have heard that right. "A secret basement full of sex furniture?" Repeating the words made it sound even more ludicrous.

Kandace grinned. "Yes. Do you want to go in? He's opened it all up to the public. It's part of his stock."

I was so very tempted. But if I looked, I might have to buy a piece or two, and then I might want to use it, and my current situation...

I pushed aside the teasing images of Kandace on a spanking bench, and shoved even harder at the sudden but enticing thought of Austin taking me on a fainting couch. *Fuck*.

"Maybe another night." Definitely another night. "You know a lot about this place."

"Our social media manager lives out here. And one of the partners grew up here—the guy loaning us the house. His name is on the town, but don't remind him of that."

I was a little in awe. "You know all the interesting people."

"Between you and Joystick, I do now," Kandace said.

I didn't have a response. "You said something about a record store?" The awning above called this The Cat's Chaotic Cacophony. I studied the large windows that were filled with vinyl, cd's, and so much music paraphernalia. "I can't believe a place like this still exists."

"Onyx is really passionate about his music." Kandace leaned some of her weight against me, her shoulder pressing into mine. Despite the coats between us, I swore I felt her heat searing into my skin. "I kind of wish he would re-open the diner next door, but that was his dad's thing, not his."

My gaze drifted to the empty building. Unlike the

other abandoned shops, this one still had some life in it. "Is he remodeling?"

Kandace nodded. "Fixing it up to sell."

"Wouldn't it be amazing if Austin set up shop there?" I was surprised at my own idea.

Because if he was there, that meant he'd stay here. And I'd go back to California.

That was bad.

No, that was exactly what should happen, wasn't it?

"Hmm." Kandace's reply was hard to read. "I'll mention it to him. He and Onyx would probably get along great, and music is another branch of great geekdom..."

As I studied her, I could almost see the gears turning in her head. So sexy. I was about to suggest we pick a place for dinner, when I heard,

"Elijah." The voice was feminine and heavily accented.

Kandace and I turned to see Isabella approaching.

"Ciao." Isabella stopped closer to me than I was comfortable with, a sweet smile in place. "I'm so happy to see a friendly face out here." She must be having a hard time fitting in.

"Isabella, hi." I tended to be polite with the actors, but not friendly. Another day I might offer to show her around, but tonight I was going to be selfish with my Kandace time. Still, introductions were appropriate. "This is Kandace. Andrew's sister. My date."

"Hi." Kandace's greeting was too bright as she extended her hand.

Isabella didn't so much as glance at her. "You're busy? I was hoping you'd have time for me." Isabella stepped even closer to me.

I wasn't playing whatever bullshit game this was. I'd spent enough time in Hollywood to be unimpressed. "No. I'm out with my girlfriend." I wrapped an arm around Kandace's waist. "But you and I can catch up on Monday."

Like that, Isabella's pleasant mask vanished—at least she was a better actress on set. "I see. Good night." She spun on her toe and walked away.

"Is *she* in Andrew's movie?" Kandace asked when Isabella was out of earshot.

"Yeah. She's playing Tara." I'd rather gloss over the whole weird and random encounter. "Do you want to go get dinner?"

Kandace's gaze was still fixed on Isabella's back as the other woman vanished into the light crowds. "Dinner sounds great." Her tone held an edge.

Given the random flash of an encounter, I didn't blame her. It was uncomfortable and obnoxious. But I was happy to spend the rest of the night assuring Kandace she was the only woman who had my attention.

20
kandace

I'D STARTED the day focused on this afternoon and this evening. On the hope—even though I shouldn't be thinking that way—that I wouldn't have to pick between Eli and Joystick.

And now that I was actually out with Eli, we'd been having so much fun all the way up to meeting Isabella. She was gone, shooed away by him, but the strange encounter had moved into my head. As Eli and I continued our stroll toward the restaurant, I tried to grasp more tidbits of information about the town, to continue our tour.

It wasn't happening.

Carly had mentioned the woman who was Diego and Raul's ex-wife a few times. Carly didn't speak about Isabella in any good terms, and I didn't blame her. The ex had abandoned her daughter as a baby, and came back into their lives after more than five years gone, claiming she'd just wanted to see her daughter.

It sounded like a mother with regrets, turning her life around.

Except that apparently Isabella really wanted access to Raul's family ties and money, and wasn't interested in her own baby girl at all.

This couldn't be the same woman, though. Could it? Here on the other side of the world, cast in a movie to play the part of her ex-husband's cousin, looking just like Carly had described, down to the snooty tone and stunning accent?

Which was harder to believe—that it was really the same Isabella or that it was a coincidence?

I could probably confirm with Carly somehow, but if I said something to Eli and wasn't sure, it could color his opinion of what might be a stranger, and make things tense for him for no reason.

What should I do? Did I need to *do* anything? *Hey, Eli. That woman you're working with might or might not be a rude, snooty, neglectful woman who tricked Joystick into flying her to Italy so she could gold dig a little.*

He worked in Hollywood. He probably encountered people like that on a regular basis.

"Earth to Kandace." Eli's tone was playful as he stepped into my path. He placed a finger under my chin and tilted my head up, to search my face. "Where'd you go?"

I tried to give a reassuring laugh, but it came out sounding forced. "I'm right here."

"Not so sure about that. You seem lost in your own head. It wasn't Isabella, was it? She's gone now."

"I know, but pushy, rude people like that..." I didn't know what to say. "I guess she kind of left an air of killed mood in her wake."

The way Eli dragged a thumb along my bottom lip sent shivers up my spine that shook away the lingering meh. "She's like so many of the others—anything she said, anything she did, it doesn't matter. She's not worth the wasted thought."

I could sink into his soft touch all night. Especially if it turned harder as things went on. "You're right." And even if that was the same Isabella that Carly talked about—it seemed like too much of a coincidence for her to not be—I wasn't going to ruin a good night because of her.

We resumed walking again, and stopped a few doors down in front of a pizza place. Lyndsay had told me I had to try it, and that I *definitely needed to avoid that big pizza chain down the street*. Eli had heard something similar from the film crew, so we decided to stop for dinner.

It was cozy inside—dim lighting, low hanging lamps over wood tables, and an actual jukebox in the corner that looked like it had been there since the town was founded more than a hundred years ago. I realized jukeboxes hadn't been around this long, but maybe this was the first ever.

We ordered food, grabbed our drinks, and found a

table. Eli held out my chair and scooted it in for me as I sat, before taking the spot across from me.

This was so *normal*. Or might be if we were sixteen and high school sweethearts. Then again, my teenage years weren't really like this. I was so focused on school, on basically raising Andrew, that I didn't really date. Not much after, either. I loved this.

"You react so differently to celebrities than most people," I said.

Eli fiddled with his straw wrapper. "Growing up around it, I figured out they were people too. Some of them are assholes, some are sweet, and most are like that Isabella woman—as fake as bad CGI."

Great analogy. "Now I'm curious, is there anyone you *would* go gaga over?"

"I don't name drop. It's tacky."

It had its time and place, but I liked his humility. "This isn't name dropping, because the assumption is you haven't met them yet. Besides, I asked you."

"I have met him, but I'd still be star struck if I ever ran into him again."

Our waitress arrived with our pizza, set it on a raised tray between us, and handed us both plates. The scent was heavenly, and Eli made sure I picked my piece first.

We were both silent for a moment, aside from moans and sighs of appreciation as we dug into some heavenly pizza.

"I still want to hear your answer," I said to Eli.

He put down his slice and washed down his bite with a swig of soda.

I was starting to think this should be one hell of a story.

"You know the guy in the action movies? *They killed my dog and stole my car*? And then he burns down an entire underground crime ring?

An actor I'd crushed on longer than those movies had been around. "I'm at least a little familiar with his work."

"I auditioned to be Chas in Constantine."

"I love that movie." Wait. I was trying to picture Eli in the role. How long ago was that? Ten years? Fifteen? On second thought, I'd rather not imagine him that young when I would've been twice his age. "You weren't old enough to drive a cab back then." Damn me and my mathy brain.

"No. In fact, they told me—he told me—that was why I didn't get the part. They went with an older character."

He told Eli… "Is that normal? For the star to call you with notes?"

"Also no. Okay, here's the setup. I was all of almost fifteen, and comics were my life, especially the dark ones." A frown whispered across his face, becoming an almost smile before it vanished. "Austin and I would hide the graphic novel collections in different places around the set. If you pay close enough attention to some of the episodes of *Donovan*, you can see the different covers tucked away. Editing tried to take out every instance, but I know where I hid the books, so I know where to look for them on the screen."

That was adorable. It also meant, "You still watch the show sometimes?"

"Sometimes. There are a couple of episodes that remind me..." He sighed. "Anyway, Austin and I would read between takes, and Hellblazer was like nothing else. Magic guy who fights demons—both real and his own personal darkness. It wasn't *good always triumphs* or *there's a distinct line between light and dark*. It was complex and real and to young me, it was brilliant.

"I devoured those stories. I'd make Austin read them out loud, and told him it was because he was a slower reader than me. It wasn't. It was completely because he was so good at slipping into each role. He was a one-man acting troupe." Eli was definitely smiling, falling into the memory.

I was captivated by both the tale and his reactions. He looked so sweet talking about Joystick that way. When the animosity faded, it was clear Eli still adored him. How was someone supposed to compete with that kind of decades of longing?

Not that I had to.

Eli gave a brief shake of his head. "When I found out I'd gotten the audition, I was sure they'd made a mistake. They must want Austin instead, and I was assured that no, they wanted the smart sassy one who gets left behind a little too much, but in the end helps save the day."

"Not the greatest way to describe someone."

Sadness tinged Eli's smile. "I knew who I was and who I was playing, and I knew those were the parts waiting for me. Back then..." He puffed out his cheeks and they deflated with his sigh. "As long as I got to do it with Austin by my side, I was okay with it. I didn't want to be the star, but to play across from *him*"—the way Eli said it, it sounded like he was actually talking about a god, rather than a time-traveling airhead turned world-class assassin.

"It didn't matter that he was almost thirty years older than me, he was so sexy in person," Eli said. "So nice. I'm still surprised I made it through my lines, and when I was done I walked out of that building on a cloud of air and fantasy. I was going to get that part. He'd take me under his wing and be my mentor. He'd have to be okay with Austin too, because I was going to love both of them... But I wouldn't put him in an awkward situation. I'd wait until I was an adult to tell Mr. Constantine that I loved him."

I was wrapped up in the story. In the highs and lows of a simple audition, through young Eli's eyes. Though, obviously he hadn't gotten the part.

"A few days later, he called me himself. Said I shouldn't expect personal feedback going forward because most casting calls didn't care about who they spit through the grinder. But he said he wished he'd had at least a little input when he was my age, so he wanted to offer it. He told me I was great, and I should be proud of my audition. That the only reason they didn't pick me was because they needed someone just a little older."

"That was really sweet of him." I was almost smitten with the story.

Eli finished off his slice. "Like I said—great guy. I've only talked to him once since then. He called me after..." The lines in Eli's forehead cut deep with the frown. "After I was forced off *Donovan*. I couldn't get an audition anywhere, and I was so frustrated. I didn't realize at the time that I'd basically been black-balled, and he told me. Said he'd overheard a director friend and remembered my name. He offered me an apology and said he wished he could help. I didn't blame him for not being able to. I thanked him. I hung up. I cried for a week at the realization of how deep Austin's betrayal ran, and decided to quit acting."

My heart ached for Eli. What was I supposed to say to something like that? *I'm sorry* hardly seemed adequate. I settled for squeezing his hand.

He squeezed back and gave me a weak smile. "A few years after that, I got a call from someone who worked with him—Constantine, not Austin. The guy had heard I was writing. Something I'd mentioned in passing, eons ago, during my Chas audition. They brought me in to be part of a team patching up a screenplay that a director hated, and that was how I got into what I do now. So yeah, if I ever meet him again, I'll go gaga over him."

Wow. That was one hell of a ride. "I get why. And I'm so sorry you went through all of that."

"It's okay. For a long time I thought it wasn't—you probably couldn't tell, but I held onto that animosity for a long time." Eli winked at me. "I convinced myself I was over it, and it's been jarring realizing that I wasn't, and that all this time, my blame was misplaced."

"Joystick has a way of shifting people's perspectives." At least, he had mine. Was it okay for me to say that now?

Eli's smile was coming back, so probably. "He's always been like that." He gave another one of those head shakes that looked like he was trying to clear out his thoughts. "But so do you."

What? How did I become a part of this? "I've actually made a career out of convincing others that old people can be fun too." I didn't mean for the self-effacing to slip out, but it forced its way past my lips. I was closer to Constantine's age than Eli's, and couldn't help thinking about what I'd been doing when he wasn't even old enough to drive. I should stop myself now, but more words wanted to be heard. "That's not true. I wasn't fun at all before—"

"Hey." Eli's voice was sharp, and he grasped the fingers of both of my hands between his. "Look at me."

Weird command, but I didn't dare obey. After that super sweet story, after seeing Eli's hurt when he talked about Austin, and the confession that they still meant that much to each other…

"Kandace." Eli's tone turned soft and coaxing.

I forced my gaze up to find him watching me with gorgeous, smart, soulful eyes.

He searched my face. "There's a hole in my soul that's Austin-shaped, and I've tried to ignore it for a long time. I don't think I can anymore and… I should really be telling him this, not you. What you need to know is that after the last few weeks, a Kandace-shaped spot has appeared in my heart. Is that sappy?"

Fluttery butterflies danced in my stomach and chest. They didn't erase the self-doubt, but they muted it. "In the best possible way."

"I don't look at you and see a number—your age or mine or the difference between the two. You're Kandace. *My* Kandace. Probably Austin's too, but he has to tell you that himself. Come here." Eli stood and tugged me to my feet.

I was too dumbstruck by his words to argue, though I did think it was odd when he led me toward the bathroom. There was only the one, and it was a larger restroom with no stalls and only one set of facilities.

Eli locked the door behind us, and my pulse skipped. What was he up to? He placed his hands on my hips and faced me toward the mirror.

Reluctance replaced anticipation, and I couldn't make myself look up.

Eli rested his finger under my chin, pressing into

my back, and forced my gaze to our reflection. I didn't recognize the woman who stared back, though I was very familiar with the man behind her. The gorgeous younger man with the kind eyes.

Vibrant hair framed my face, and my cheeks were flushed pink.

Eli's eyes met mine in the mirror. He tucked my hair behind one ear, and brushed his lips along the shell of said ear. "You are stunning. Smart. Funny." He trailed his fingers down my cheek to my neck, sending shivers up my spine. "You're the perfect amount of adventurous for me. Can you see that?"

"I just see me. Not the person you're describing." That wasn't completely true, though. I didn't know how to say what I was thinking. I did see me, but it was the me I thought I was when I was younger. The me I'd given up on after so long of not being able to embrace her.

"*Just* you is the most amazing woman." He nipped at my earlobe and kissed a trail down my neck, and I tilted my head for more of his touch. "And if you don't see it, I'll have to keep seeing it for both of us." His breath, his words, were hot on my skin.

He drew his fingers down my front, brushing my bare skin before he reached the collar of my blouse, and undoing buttons as his touch traveled further down.

We shouldn't do this here, but it all felt incredible. Intoxicating.

When he tugged open the edges of my shirt,

enough to expose more of my skin to our reflections, I nearly pulled the top closed again. I didn't want to see myself glaring back at me—the hints of less than perfect skin. The handles of pudge hanging over the waist of my trousers.

Eli grabbed my wrists, stopping me from covering up. "I adore what I see—who I see—when I look at you," he said, and pulled my arms behind me, to capture both with one hand. His other palm moved to my stomach, and slid up toward my bra. "I fantasize about the things I'm going to do with you. The conversations we'll have. The sex." He traced a light touch over lace, over one of my nipples, and a zing of desire shocked me.

I would protest any of this, but I was too focused on enjoying it all. On sinking into the contact and the flattery.

He let go of my wrists, though they were still mostly trapped between him and me, and moved both of his hands to the bottom of my bra, shoving it up to free my breasts.

I gasped in shock and at the cool brush of air from being exposed. Heat replaced chill as he cupped me, and rolled my nipples between his fingers. I should stop him, but I didn't want to.

"I've been dreaming for days about how I was going to elicit that orgasm you owe me." His voice was low and tempting, rolling over me and mixing with his teasing.

I didn't have any sort of brilliant comeback. "Me too."

"I'm thinking here and now is a solid idea." Eli pressed more of his body against mine, while he continued to knead my breasts and suck on my skin. His erection was distinct against the small of my back. "Did I say solid? I meant hard."

I wasn't about to point out that didn't make sense. "What if someone hears us?" My heart hammered against my ribs and I squirmed from his touch.

With a playful huff, he bit the crook where my neck met my shoulder, then pressed his lips to my skin. "You'd better either be quiet, or be prepared for them to hear. Because if I have to make you come in a public bathroom, to prove to you how irresistible you are, I will."

Who was I to protest that kind of resolve? Besides, this felt naughty in all the best ways.

I was so drawn into his touch, that I had to bite the inside of my cheek to keep the squeaks and sighs from escaping, and he teased me until clenching my thighs together didn't sate the need.

When Eli unbuttoned my pants, yanked open my zipper, my anticipation skyrocketed. He pushed my trousers and panties down to my knees, and slipped one hand between my legs to tease my opening while he continued to kiss and bite along my neck.

I couldn't do much with my back to him, with my clothing in this state, except grind against him. I needed more. Him inside me. Release from this building need.

He nudged me forward, urging me to bend at the waist, making me catch myself on the sink. The tear of foil was a new harmony to accompany my thumping pulse. The feeling of his cock nudging my entrance was a new verse. The way he slipped inside me, stretching me out…

So, so good. If I died in here—because God knew my heart was beating fast enough—at least I'd pass on happy.

When Eli was buried inside me, he slipped his fingers to my clit. He moved in and out of me at a slow, steady pace, while he stroked the aching bud between my legs. I was already so slick with anticipation, so close to bursting, that it didn't take much to push me over the edge.

As climax spread through me, stealing my thoughts and breath, Eli gripped my hips with sticky fingers, and the slow steady build vanished in a frantic, hard pounding.

I barely held onto the thought *keep quiet*, but the rest of my restraint was gone. Climax engulfed me, and I clenched around him as he fucked me with a fast intensity that was all-consuming.

His grunts, the way his rhythm changed, made me think he was close too. I couldn't help but watch in the mirror, the way his face screwed up as he came. The way he jerked in time with his muffled grunts and groans.

As we both slowed to a stop, only our breathing, mingled with a fan, filled the room.

I managed to find my voice. "Did you bring me in here just for this?" I teased.

"No." There was a growl in his voice that hadn't been there before. "I brought you in here to show you the woman I see when I look at you. But then inspiration struck."

"Chasing the inspiration. That's what makes you a great storyteller."

This time his kisses along the back of my neck were more tender. "Maybe, maybe not. But chasing you has made me feel more complete than I've felt... ever."

I didn't think I could put my thoughts and feelings into such sweet words, and I felt silly parroting him, but I had to say something. I rested more of my weight against him. "Me too."

21
kandace

My FACE WAS HOT, my pulse was racing, and giddiness spilled through my veins as Eli and I returned to the dining room. Could anyone tell what we'd done? If they could, did it matter?

"Do you want to go home?" Eli wrapped an arm around my waist and nudged me back to our table.

The city tour was fun, but the intimacy with him was better. Not just the naughty orgasm in the bathroom, but all of it. "Joystick is home." I hated to risk ruining the moment, but it seemed like something that needed to be said.

"He is. We could bring him some food, since he missed out on the fun."

Whatever switch was flipping between them, I both liked it and was a little scared of it. Would I be as much fun for them once they cleared away all the debris from their past?

Eli's words, his touch, from the bathroom still

lingered in my head, and I clung to the memory. Of course I was still a part of all of this. "Sounds like a plan. Let's do it."

We had them box up the leftover pizza, and were on our way.

Eli and I made our way back to the house, a comfortable silence settling between us. His arm pressed into mine as we walked, and a moment later, he tangled his fingers with mine. The warmth that spread through me this time wasn't arousal, but it was definitely desire. This felt so sweetly perfect.

Except for that stupid bit of my mind that insisted I couldn't have it all, no matter how sweet both men were. Why exactly was I convinced of that?

Because that was what it had been my entire life. Always the bridesmaid, never the bride, as they said. Why would now be the moment that not one, but two, wonderful men decided they were willing to put aside years of animosity, angst, and obvious attraction, to include me in their lives long term?

Eli squeezed my hand as we drew closer to the house. He met me before he knew I had anything to do with Joystick. He showed an interest in me, asked me out…

I knew he was sincere, but that nagging insecure voice, the one that had been left at the metaphorical roadside too many times, didn't want to get hurt again. I'd *known* with past boyfriends, too.

We stepped inside the house and found Joystick waiting on the couch. The scent in the room was different from when we left—spice and vinegar and meat.

He looked up the moment the door opened, and grinned. "Welcome back, you crazy kids. How was it?"

"Dinner was so good we brought you your own serving." Eli held up the take-out box, and sniffed the air. "I think you may have eaten already."

"I just whipped up some wings real quick. I was hungry and I've been wanting to try out a new recipe."

Those words were said too casually given their meaning. *"Whipped up some wings?"* I repeated.

Eli frowned. "You're supposed to be staying off that foot."

"Sorry, *Dad*." Joystick's voice was playful. "I promise I hobbled to the kitchen, and sat most of the time. Very little standing involved."

"Were they good? The wings?" I should've guessed he could cook, too, since he wanted to open a restaurant. But I hadn't even considered that was one more thing Joystick could do.

He shrugged. "Not the best, but they're getting there. Thank you for the food though. We can heat it up later and share it." He scooted closer to the arm of the couch, and patted the seat next to him. "You should both sit down. Talk a while. Tell me about your night, except maybe any of the kissy bits. Unless you want to tell me, then I'm all ears."

Right. The yummy kissy, fucky bits that happened

in a restaurant bathroom. That was going to be a favorite memory forever.

Eli left the space in the middle for me, and Joystick tugged me into the spot with no hesitation. They weren't acting like two men who didn't want me around, or who only wanted each other.

And being pressed between them like this was cozy and comfortable. It felt right.

"So, what did you do? Where did you go? Did you have a lot of fun?" Joystick was a lot of things, but politeness for the sake of politeness didn't seem to be one of them. Was it weird that we were having this casual conversation?

Was it possible I could just stop over-thinking things now, please?

"We had a *lot* of fun," Eli said.

"Except when we ran into one of the actresses from his movie." What was wrong with me?

Though, if anyone could tell me if that was *the* Isabella, it was Joystick. She was the reason he'd gone to Italy in the first place so many months ago. The story was he'd met her at a party, gotten really drunk, and when the pretty woman said *I need to go save my daughter*, he had them on a flight to Milan a few hours later.

"Anyone you knew? Anyone I know?" Joystick asked.

Eli found my hand again, and rested both his and mine on my knee. "She's working on the movie, so yeah, I know her. Not sure you would. I think she's pretty new to the US scene. She's an Italian actress."

"Named Isabella," I added.

Joystick raised an eyebrow. "Really." That was possibly the most serious look I'd ever seen him adopt.

I had to make him understand it was even more of a coincidence than he realized. "A little backstory, since you're probably not as familiar with Andrew's screenplay as Eli is... Andrew spent his late teens and early twenties backpacking around the world, and he spent some time in Italy in the process. Where he met two of his still good friends, Antonio and Tara." Brother and sister. And Raul's cousins. "She's playing Tara in the movie."

"Really." Joystick repeated. "What's she like?"

"Petit. Pretty. Snooty." I wasn't being catty, or maybe just a little, but I'd also just described a quarter of the population. Not helpful.

Joystick had his phone in his hand and was jabbing at the screen. He turned it toward both of us a moment later, and showed us a celebrity gossip webpage with a photo of the woman we'd encountered this evening, her arm looped through his. "Is that her?"

I swallowed the bubble of jealousy that swelled in my throat and the sight of her clinging to Joystick that way. The possessive mewl of *mine* that echoed in my thoughts wasn't so easily ignored.

"That's her," Eli said. "Do you know everyone I've met in the last few months?"

"I don't know Andrew. I'd like to. Sounds like a fascinating guy. Then again," Joystick leaned his head on my shoulder, "I'm interested in meeting everyone in your life."

Hear that, brain? That's not him just being nice.

My brain scoffed at me.

"But if what you're saying is true..." Eli twisted his face. "And I don't know why you would make it up, why would she be here? Isn't that kind of a big coincidence?"

Joystick sucked in a sharp breath through his teeth. "So, I may have possibly, probably, talked a lot about you, Eli, when I was around her. Not that I remember specifically doing that, but it's a thing I tend to do."

"You tend to talk about me."

"Yup."

According to Carly, that had become my role when Joystick was spending time with Diego and Raul—the person Joystick talked about a lot. Before that, he was prone to bring up a man he hadn't seen for fifteen years? Who hated his guts on principle until a week or so ago?

"You didn't do that to Kandace did you?" Eli's question was laced with concern and pending anger.

"She and I didn't do much talking—"

"Uh-uh." Eli cut him off. "Kandace didn't go back

to some stranger's room who wasn't stimulating her mentally."

Eli was right. Even this new, wilder Kandace would've been put off by a Joystick who couldn't hold up a good conversation. He didn't remember the night differently, did he? "No, I wouldn't have. There was definitely talking first, and no, he didn't mention Eli."

Joystick screwed his face up and furrowed his brows. "Then I guess with Isabella… I was comparing her to the one great relationship I'd had before her. I did that a lot."

"And then you met Kandace and replaced me?" Was that actual teasing in Eli's voice? Playfulness? What was happening here, because it felt good.

Joystick shifted his weight on the couch as much as he could with the cast on, and looked at me, then past me to Eli, then at me again. "Neither of you replaced the other. I want you both."

His words were both as sweet and as terrifying as what Eli said earlier.

"I reached the same conclusion not too long ago," Eli said with a light chuckle.

Joystick grinned. "What about you, Kandace?"

My turn. This was my chance to confess I hoped for the same thing. The words were in my brain, and I'd thought them over and over. Why were they lodged in my throat now? "How's a woman supposed to complain about that?"

Both men looked satisfied with my answer, but the entire conversation left my brain warring with itself.

It was easy to forget my doubts though as the night and the conversation flowed on. Then again, a lot of things were easy with the two of them. Joystick made it easy to relax and forget anything bad had ever existed, and Eli made it easy to think. To question things from new angles. Both of them let me see the world differently, and I liked their perspectives.

At some point, Joystick couldn't shrug off his winces anymore, and we made him admit that his ankle was starting to bother him. We all moved into the bedroom, to let him lie down and prop up his foot.

He insisted we stay and keep him company, and that he wasn't going to lay in the bed alone and be bored. We were going to join him.

I was fine with that. It was a comfy, intimate space to sit while we talked about everything from script writing to sitting in the make-up chair to discovering the secrets of the universe.

"OH, HOLY SHIT." Lucas's shocked tone yanked me from sleep.

I was pressed between Joystick and Eli, in Joystick's bed. We were all still fully clothed, which made sense because according to the memories floating back, we'd made our way in here last night, and fallen asleep talking.

Was guilt making me dream that my son had caught us like this?

"I'm walking away now," Lucas said.

Damn it. He was actually here, standing in the doorway to the bedroom and not making any motion to leave at all. Though he did have his hand over his eyes.

"We're all dressed," I said.

He jammed his fingers in his ears and screwed his eyes shut. "La-la-la-la." He turned and walked away.

Double damn it. Joystick and Eli were both looking between me and him, with questioning expressions.

"My son." I climbed from the bed. "I have to stop him. Explain." I didn't wait for any responses as I chased Lucas down and caught him in the living room.

This was exactly what I wanted to avoid. This was why I hadn't told him... Fuck. "Wait."

"I swear to God, Mom." Lucas stared me down. "If you tell me it's not what it looks like..." His tone was flat. Emotionless.

"It depends on what it looked like. We were sleep-ing." As I stood across from him, I smoothed my clothes as best I could, and raked my fingers through my hair, which had to be a mess.

"What did you do to your hair?" Lucas's attention shifted like that.

I frowned. "Is it bad?"

"It's gorgeous, but I leave you alone for a week and I find you with purple hair and in bed with my childhood heroes?" Lucas jabbed me in the arm. "Are you a pod person?"

I lightly smacked his hand away. This playfulness was a good sign. "Stop. No. I'm still me."

"Are you sure? Because *my* mom wouldn't lie to me about sleeping with Donovan."

I winced. "Please don't call him that. It's not his name."

"What do you call him? Bad Boy Anaconda?"

Oh, Christ. "Joystick."

"Oh. My. God. *Mom*. That's not any better." Despite the shock in Lucas's voice, amusement tugged at the corners of his mouth.

"That's what I go by." Joystick's voice came from behind me.

I glanced back to see he and Eli had joined us, but had stayed closer to the bedroom, as if they weren't sure it was all right to approach.

"Would you like us to go?" Eli asked.

No. But also, maybe for just a few minutes? But no.

Joystick propelled himself forward on the crutches as if he'd been using them for years, not days. "We could keep hiding in the bedroom, but we can hear the whole conversation anyway, and it feels rude to eavesdrop."

"No, I don't want you to go." Lucas managed to

vocalize what I couldn't. "I want to meet you. *Mom*, how could you not... You know who they are, right? And you never said anything?"

Introductions, I could do that. "Joystick, Eli, this is my son Lucas. He's one of your biggest fans." It hadn't been too long ago when mentioning that would have killed any mood in the room. Not that there was much to worry about there right now.

"*Biggest* fan," Lucas corrected me. "Except my mom, apparently. You were in bed with them." He looked at me again.

"We were just sleeping."

"This time," Joystick said.

I shot him a look, and his smirk implied he wasn't sorry.

"I can go pick us up some breakfast. I'll take Austin with me." Bless Eli.

Apparently it was possible for Lucas to look more incredulous. "*We'll go get breakfast*. How long have you known them? What happened to his foot? How did you keep all of this a secret?"

"I'm dating them." That probably wasn't the most tactful answer I could've come up with, but I was running out of filters.

"Both of them?"

"Yes." Eli and Joystick answered at the same time.

Okay, so that filled me with lots of warm fuzzies regardless of the situation.

Lucas sank into the nearest chair. "I mean, it's not

winning the lottery, and it's not why I ever pictured calling either of you *Daddy*—"

"Lucas." Warm fuzzies gone. Hello, utter embarrassment.

"What? I was going to say this was still pretty damn epic," Lucas said. "Oh, by the way, my car died at the edge of town."

What? "You didn't mention that up front?"

"Cars can be repaired. But this may be the only time I walk in on my mom in bed with *Joystick and Eli.*" Lucas stood again. "I'm still processing the awesome."

Sometimes this boy had Andrew's priorities. "So where's your car now," I asked. "And while we're on the subject, why are you here, and how did you get into the house?"

Lucas shrugged. "Andrew asked me to bring him something. Car died. Some sexy old guy was driving by in an Impala, gave me a ride there then here, and a key to the house."

"*Sexy old guy?*" I repeated. "*God.* Please don't tell me you called Xander that to his face."

"Give me some credit. I only thought about saying that to his face. How about I go find the car repair place, pick us up breakfast, and while I'm gone the three of you can get your story straight. I'm taking your car, by the way."

I had no idea when he'd grabbed my keys, but my purse was in plain view, so it wasn't a big mystery how. "You sound too much like Andrew sometimes." I didn't mean it in a bad way.

Lucas didn't look bothered. "You'd better tell a better story than he does."

"I promise you that Eli is a better storyteller." Though I may be a little biased. A lot.

Lucas pulled out his phone. "You don't even call them by their full names. You're just like *Joystick. Eli.* Like it's the most natural thing in the world. I'm literally deceased right now."

"You're not, because you're still standing here talking. Breakfast?" I'd like to move past this moment in life. It went far better than expected though. Enough that if I shoved aside the embarrassment, I was pretty pleased with the whole thing.

Lucas jabbed his phone a few times. "Rawr, I'm a zombie. I'm going though. What's everyone eating?" He took our orders, and walked out of the house mumbling, "I'm buying breakfast for fucking Donavan and Corey. My mom is *fucking* Donovan and Corey."

"I like him," Joystick said the moment the door closed.

"This feels weird to say—the words, not what they mean—but I agree with Austin."

That definitely went better than I expected. This whole morning was strange, but was it a bad strange?

22
joystick

WATCHING Kandace interact with her son, the easy friendship they had, made me realize something.

It was possible to adore her more.

It did remind me though, I'd been curious about something in regards to Lucas. It never seemed like a good time to ask, but I'd rather know now if the topic was off-limits. "Lucas's father. Is he out of the picture?" I asked Kandace. "You don't have to share any messy details, but divorce? Death? One night stand...?"

"None of the above. Not for me, anyway. One night stand, I suppose. And no, his biological father is very much a part of his life."

Jealousy flashed inside, but I suppressed it. I'd never once heard her mention the man. What was that look on Eli's face? "Are you smirking?"

"No." Eli's expression went blank and he shrugged.

As I looked between them, something else occurred to me. "I'm the only one who doesn't know this story."

"Andrew's his father," Kandace said.

That damn grin of Eli's was back. Though it was better than his scowl. "You know how that sounds, don't you?"

My brain had glitched. Kandace— She hadn't— "I don't— Your brother? That Andrew?"

"This is why I don't talk about it." Kandace didn't sound upset at all. "I'm not Lucas's birth mother. Andrew got a girl pregnant and didn't know. He was in South America when she dropped newborn Lucas on my doorstep, and there was no way I was letting someone else raise that innocent little child. Especially not my brother, who was barely more than a baby himself. Lucas knows the truth, we told him seven or eight years ago, but I'm Mom and my brother is Uncle Andrew."

That made so much more sense. "Then the whole thing isn't as nearly we-must-protect-the-bloodline as it sounds."

Kandace seemed to consider this. "I suppose in a way... But no. Do I have something on my face?"

"No." I should stop staring. "I just hadn't realized it was possible to like you more." Especially comparing her to someone like Isabella. When I'd realized she was only in Italy for her baby daddys' money and connections I'd been so furious. Kandace was in a different realm. "You're incredible in every way."

"Not in every way. I do have some flaws."

"But even those are good." Eli's words echoed my thoughts.

An exaggerated gagging sound broke through the conversation. "Do you want me to come back?" Lucas had returned.

"As long as you take their attention off me, you can stay." Kandace's reply was a blend of teasing and serious.

"Pft." Lucas set two take-out bags on the table. "I already know about my mom. I want to know about you guys."

I was one of my favorite subjects.

Kandace was already handing out boxes. "Tell him to stop if he makes you uncomfortable."

Seemed unlikely. "I don't really get uncomfortable," I said.

"We noticed." Eli winked.

"So are you or are you not secret lovers who have been married, secretly, in secret since Corey left the show?" Lucas asked.

I hid my wince and braced myself for Eli's reaction. I'd been wrong—this made me uncomfortable.

Kandace's grimace shone through loud and clear. "You don't open a conversation that way. We should eat before the food gets cold."

"What?" Lucas didn't look fazed. "Of course I'm going to ask the tough questions up front."

"It's okay." At Eli's assurance, some of the tension drained from the room, and hope sparked inside me. "And no, is the answer to your question," he said. "Austin and I haven't spoken for more than a decade, up until a week or two ago."

Lucas looked between Eli and me. "And...?"

"You want the full story, you'll have to buy the book." My flippant answer came easily. Probably not the best way to move the conversation along.

Especially the way Lucas's eyes grew wide. "There's going to be a book?"

Kandace's shock turned to an adorable smirk as she opened the takeout bag and began to extract boxes.

Lucas lightly smacked her hand. "No working for you. Sit down next to your *boyfriends*, and I'll take care of this."

Kandace raised her brows, but complied, taking a seat between Eli and me.

"There should be a book." The more I thought about it, the more I liked it. The *real* Donovan and Corey story. No. Wait. That was too rhymey.

Eli rolled his eyes, but he didn't look upset. "Are you going to write it?"

"Hello. I'm not the writer." Duh.

"No, there's not going to be a book." Eli shook his head. "My half of the story would be dull as all get out and Austin's half is already online for the world to see."

"But I want the secret, sordid stuff that people

speculate about but never really get to hear," Lucas handed me a box, then Eli, and Kandace.

He expected drama, and would probably be super disappointed with the truth.

"You don't want the secret, sordid stuff," Eli assured him.

Lucas extracted the last box, crumpled the plastic, and tossed it away. "Yes I do."

No. He didn't. "It involves your mom," I said.

With a huff, he sank into his seat. "Not *that* sordid stuff." His pout looked exaggerated. "I want the *gay* stuff."

"I'm sure there are deep fakes online that will give you exactly what you're looking for." Eli's answer surprised me.

Not because he was wrong, but because I didn't think that was something he'd willingly admit.

"Eat." Kandace tapped the top of Lucas's box. "And tell me what happened to your car, and if someone is taking care of it."

It was such a normal thing. A mom looking out for her kid. And seeing how easily Lucas and Kandace got along, how natural their relationship was, made me smile. It was cute and it was sweet.

And I was glad she wasn't stopping us from talking to him. All the angst and sexiness and everything in between was incredible, but this meant maybe she was ready to admit we would be good for her long term. That Kandace, Eli, and I could last.

We all dug into our food. Kandace poked Lucas as

he shoveled eggs into his mouth. "Slow down and eat like a human being."

His flush was reminiscent of hers. *"Mom."* Amazing how much embarrassment could be carried in a single syllable. Lucas swallowed hard and gulped down juice. "Don't know what's wrong with my car, but Cash said water pump maybe."

"Cash?" I repeated.

"So get this, the auto repair place is called Johnny's, and the guy who owns it is Cash. That's the kind of shit that's too implausible to make up." Lucas grinned.

He had a point.

"I'm just glad it died so close to town," Kandace said. "And that Xander happened by."

"I was about to call Triple-A. It wasn't like I would've been stranded."

The way Lucas was inhaling his food had me reminiscing about the joys of being more than ten years younger. Those thoughts led a little further back to Eli, and I couldn't help but glance at him. It was almost surreal that after so long, he was here. That we'd both met Kandace. That all three of us were so perfect together.

We wrapped up our breakfast with more random conversation, and Lucas insisted on cleaning up while we moved back into the living room.

When Kandace explained that she and I were waiting on Lyndsay, and were going to do *actual work*, Lucas twisted his mouth. "It's Saturday. Boring."

"Take Eli to Deacon's," Kandace suggested. "We didn't get a chance to go last night, and he might like the basement."

The face Lucas made was somewhere between horror and humiliation. "Eww. No."

"Who's Deacon? What's in his basement?" I looked between them.

Eli didn't look confused at all. "That's the one you said had the basement—"

"Ugh. Gross." Lucas jammed his fingers in his ears.

That seemed to amuse Eli even more. "You said you wanted to know about the gay stuff."

"And pretend I didn't find you both in bed *with my mom*."

"Rumor is, Deacon has a large quantity of sexy antique furniture." Eli finally filled me in.

"It's not just a rumor. It's true." As we returned to the living room, Kandace grabbed her laptop.

I liked the idea of sexy furniture, regardless of how old it was. "I'm going to have to check that out."

Lucas shook his head. "I'm going to the bookstore to wait for my car. It should be safe and not nearly so scarring there."

"I'll go with Lucas," Eli said. "Let the two of you work." The doorbell rang. "Or, I'll get that." He crossed the room, and opened the door.

"Hi, I'm looking for Kand..." The woman trailed off as she looked past Eli and her gaze fell on us.

"This is not what you told me I was signing up for." Her pleasant tone shifted to frustrated in a blink.

Kandace furrowed her brow. "I was pretty clear when we talked yesterday."

"Not about this." The new arrival pulled out her phone. "He is going to be a lot more effort than you said."

I didn't like the way she said *he* or that she kept glancing at me with a frown. "Am I a problem?"

"For me personally? Depends on how much of this is true. For the rest of the world? You're a problem."

What the fuck?

"Eli, Joystick, this is Lyndsay. She's not usually so grumpy or judgmental," Kandace said.

Lyndsay pursed her lips. "None of you knows what I'm talking about. I'm going to assume that, instead of that you've lost all sense of reason."

What *was* she talking about? "Assume that, yes. And I'll assume what you're saying isn't personal."

Lyndsay scrolled through her phone, then crossed the room to show the screen to Kandace.

"My harrowing weekend with a former child star. The story of how the once famous abandoned me in another country and nearly cost my daughter her life." As Kandace read the words, my blood ran cold.

"By Isabella Marino." Kandace looked at me.

Her expression was impossible to read, but fury coursed through my veins.

23
elijah

KANDACE AND LYNDSAY took turns reading aloud from an article about a woman who had just wanted to go home and see her daughter. Isabella was a struggling actress who hadn't been back to her country in so long, and when she met a man at a party, he insisted he'd take her.

She hadn't wanted to accept an expensive gift like that from a stranger, but it was all in the name of seeing her baby girl.

The story quickly slid downhill from there. According to Isabella, Austin spent the first leg of the trip talking about how no one was as good as his ex-boyfriend, ˇ and when they arrived in Italy, he was rude to Eloise's father. Then the girl went missing, and Austin told Isabella she was a horrible mother and walked out on her.

On top of that, he flaunted his popularity, he slept with another woman, and he abandoned Isabella in

Italy without a way home or any way of knowing her daughter was safe.

The story also included my name, Kandace's, the firm she was a partner at, and mention of Andrew's movie.

Kandace and Lyndsay both wore scowls when they were finished.

I hated that a few weeks ago, I would've been ready to accept that entire article at face value, despite the plot holes.

"Technically, all of that is true in some way." Austin didn't sound concerned.

Lyndsay stared at him with her mouth twisted. She pointed at each person in the room, her mouth moving as she counted silently. "I'm going to say this because you brought me in for my professional advice. Never say that in front of anyone again, especially not four other someone's. I don't care if you're joking or if you mean *technically*. I assume it didn't happen the way this woman made it sound, because Kandace wouldn't work with you if you were an asshole."

I was both impressed and annoyed that Isabella had managed to drag so many of us through the mud at once, but overall, it was infuriating that whatever issues she had during her encounter with Austin, this was her version of closure.

Lyndsay scrubbed her face and sank into the nearest seat. She pulled her tablet out and a digital pencil, and sat poised and ready. "Tell me your version of the story, then we'll figure out the best approach to countering this."

"Isn't the best approach for me to tell *everyone* my version of the story?" Austin asked.

The bookstore would wait, and he knew better.

The look Lyndsay gave him implied she felt the same—he should already know the answer to that question, and it was *no*, the truth is never quite enough. "We have to make sure things are worded impeccably. Okay, that's not actually possible, but we'll get close. Tell me the real story."

Austin's version of things was much better, though I saw where the parallel's lay between his tale and Isabella's smear piece. He talked about meeting a woman at a party while he was drunk and she was drunk, and she convinced him it would be fun to fly to Italy. So he agreed.

That sounded a lot like the man I knew, had re-met recently. Impulsive, but looking to connect with people rather than hurt anyone.

When Austin sobered up, Isabella told him she hadn't seen her daughter in years and missed her. He agreed that wasn't right. The first time he met her daughter's fathers, they were rude. When the girl went missing, Isabella confessed she was really only there for their money.

And yes, Austin had insulted her and walked out at that point.

"That's horrible." Why was I the only one who

looked bothered by the story of a young girl going missing?

Austin nodded. "It was terrifying. We found her though and she was fine. Thank God."

"The good news is, your story matches Carly's," Lyndsay said.

Ah. So they already knew this one. "You didn't think Austin was lying."

Lyndsay shrugged. "I was pretty sure he wasn't an asshole. I knew the blog post was bullshit. But there's no way to tell how he remembered things. Not that the internet cares, but it's always easier to work with someone who doesn't insist on spinning everything."

We spent the next few hours doing what Lyndsay told us, everyone tag-teaming assignments to make sure Austin could handle this.

This was a side of things I never missed, being where I was in Hollywood, but for him, I didn't hesitate.

He smiled and laughed through the whole thing, but there was a thread of stress underneath, especially every time he checked into a social media account and got a glimpse of someone else tearing him down.

The one thing none of us could really help with, and I hated each time a frown whispered across his face.

Kandace fielded a handful of calls as well, all asking about her involvement. In each case, she spit out a carefully crafted response Lyndsay had given her, but she also stood by Austin without hesitation.

The longer the morning wore on, the deeper the lines in her forehead grew.

My phone chimed with a new text and I read the message aloud. "Andrew says *looks like we have to recast Tara.*"

"Not that I disagree, but does he say why?" Austin asked.

I read the follow-up note. "Because there's no way the twat who maligned my sister is working on my fucking movie." Well said.

One corner of Kandace's mouth tugged up, and the dark clouds lingering around Austin vanished with his grin.

It was a nice moment of levity, but I still hated how bad this looked for Austin. For everyone, but especially him. Because he'd done a fun, nice thing. Because he'd acted without thinking *maybe this person doesn't have the purest intentions.*

We were most of the way through distributing responses to all the right outlets, and had told Lucas multiple times that he didn't have to run and get us coffee. He didn't have to make us snacks. He was allowed to just hang out with us without being our gopher.

At the sound of the doorbell, he was on his feet in an instant. "I'll get it. If it's the paparazzi I'll tell them to fuck off."

"It's not the paparazzi." Lyndsay didn't look up from her computer. "Though, give them a couple more hours and one or two might trickle in." She glanced at Austin. "You're a massive name again. But probably not in the way you expected."

"As long as they all come to my restaurant when it opens." Austin's joke was strained.

"Hey, Cash." Lucas's greeting came from the door.

Lyndsay went about three shades paler.

"Hey. Your car's ready," a new male voice said, accompanied by the jingle of keys.

I glanced over my shoulder past Lucas to see a man with shoulders almost as broad as the doorway. He was the kind of burly I would've thrown myself at once upon a time. But he was focused on someone else. "Hey, Lynds. Didn't expect to see you here."

"My car's out front." Lyndsay's tone was hard to read.

"Is it?" Cash's surprise didn't sound sincere in any way. "Am I interrupting? Early Saturday party?" He sounded friendly. Warm.

Lucas moved aside and opened the door wider. "This is the guy I left my car with."

Cash took a step into the room.

"This is my ex-husband's brother." Lyndsay's reply explained so much about the difference in her attitude and his. She finally focused on Cash. "We're super busy right now."

Kandace crossed the room, purse in hand. "Thank you for delivering the car in person. How much do I owe you?"

"For a friend of Lyndsay's? Nothing. Besides, I had the part lying around."

Lyndsay rolled her eyes, but didn't successfully hide a soft smile.

"Absolutely not," Kandace said. "Give me a number or I'll make one up."

Cash shrugged. "Nope."

If he thought that would deter Kandace, he was about to be disappointed.

She pulled out her checkbook, scribbled, tore out the check, and handed it to him. "Thank you."

Cash glanced at the piece of paper, and then did a double take. He raised his brows. "This is at least double—"

"Then you should've given me a price." Kandace returned to her seat.

"Better take it. She can be brutally kind when she wants," Lyndsay said.

Cash folded the check once and tucked it into his shirt pocket. "I should've known that was the kind of company you'd keep." His tone was playful. "Stop by the shop when you're done?"

"It might be late."

"Stop by the house then. Generous customer gave me a huge tip. I'll buy dinner."

Lyndsay puffed out her cheeks and sighed. "No promises." Her tone had softened a great deal since he showed up though.

But as we got back to work, the somber mood returned quickly. The support was pouring in for Austin, but so was the hate. For him. For Kandace. I was used to it, and could ignore it, but this was going to impact their jobs. Their lives.

I texted Andrew back and told him I was going to be there when he fired Isabella. I needed to see that, regardless of whether I had the right to ask based on my job. His reply was a simple *Of course.*

We were wrapping up, when Austin huffed. "The amount of work Isabella is causing all of you. I swear, if I ever see her again…"

With a lot of people, I'd assume they were about to make a dangerous threat, but laugh it off as a joke. It was easy to admit now that Austin wasn't that kind of person.

"I'd kick her tires real hard with my cast." He finished the thought.

"And probably hurt yourself far more than her tire," I said.

He screwed up his face. "No. This thing is heavy. It'd probably, maybe leave a dent for like a second or two."

"No." Strict Lyndsay was back. "You can't joke about this shit, even if you think you're among friends."

I hated that she was right.

Austin's frown made me think he did as well. "If I ever see her again… I won't let her sign my cast?"

Lyndsay tilted her head back and forth. "Accept-able. Ludicrous, but acceptable."

"Can I sign your cast?" Lucas asked.

Austin held out a pen. "Duh."

Lucas grinned and knelt next to him, scribbling out a neat signature accompanied by a cartoon of a stick figure riding a corgi.

I wasn't sure if it meant anything, but it was cute, and the drawing was detailed enough I could tell what kind of dog it was.

Lucas turned to me. "Yours too."

"I'm not wearing a cast."

He nodded at the splint on my thumb. "There's tape. That'll work."

No reason to turn down such an enthusiastic offer, so I held out my thumb and Lucas left me a scribble of a kitten covered in spots. "Why do I get a cat and he gets a dog? Not that I'm complaining."

"Because that's who the two of you are." Lucas made it sound like the answer was obvious.

Which made me wonder if asking how he figured was appropriate.

We finished work, and Lyndsay told us all we could do now was watch and wait and counter anything that came up. Austin had to stick to his story no matter what.

Lucas headed out, and Lyndsay left a short while later. She could be heading home, but I suspected she was going to see Cash, based on the quiet smile playing on her face as she walked out the door.

Kandace stayed with us the rest of the weekend, but the mood was subdued. Still, having her here, having Austin here, made everything better. Even if we weren't touring the town or doing weird and wild things or fucking, their presence made me smile.

How incredible would it be to spend most of my weekends this way? To come home to them at night…

I didn't dare dream, but I also couldn't make myself stop. My brain insisted getting involved with Austin again was a mistake. Falling for a woman like Kandace who had a whole other world she belonged to, could mean heartache in the end.

But my heart was willing to take both chances to find something wonderful.

Monday morning on the set was as hectic as any other filming day. When Andrew called my name, I was happy to join him away from the chaos.

We made some idle chatter about the weather and generic comments about our weekends. Ridiculous to brush over it, given the text exchange we'd had.

"You still sticking it to my sister?" Andrew asked. "Bow-chica-bow-wow style?"

I raised my brows. "Do you really want to ask me that?"

"No. But the question makes you more uncomfortable than it does me." His answer came easily. "I actually have a great deal of respect for Kandace. She's one of the best people I've ever known."

She really was great. "You don't have to sell me, I'm already hooked," I said.

Andrew snorted a laugh. "I'm not selling you—of course you like her. I'm telling you don't hurt her. Ever."

"That's the last thing I want." I meant that more than I'd meant most anything in my life.

Andrew's phone rang and he glanced at the screen. His teasing frown became a genuine scowl. "Hang on," he said to me before answering, "Talk to me… I did. I—… No, I don't think that… I don't plan for anything to change… Why would you—… No… In that case, fuck you very much."

That went downhill fast.

"Fucking asshole." Andrew jammed his phone back into his pocket.

"What was that about?"

He let out a long sigh. "One of our bigger investors just pulled out. And not even in a sexy money-shot kind of way. Says I'm associated with Joystick, and they can't be associated with me in that case."

"Ouch."

Andrew shook his head. "Nah. We'll find a way. I don't need any of that judgmental shit backing me anyway."

It was great that he felt that way, and I respected him that much more for it, but I hated watching everyone go through this. Especially knowing that regardless of what kind of smile Austin wore, he would hate that this was bleeding into other people's lives.

24
kandace

BEFORE LUCAS CAME ALONG, and after he moved out, I'd lived alone. It wasn't a big deal—it was just the way things were.

But walking into an empty house Sunday night was one of the hardest things I'd ever done.

I hadn't known Joystick or Eli long enough to miss them this much when they weren't around, but I did anyway. But neither of them lived here. When this was over—when Joystick's ankle was healed, when the movie was done and Eli's contract was up, they were going back to their lives in other places.

It wasn't like they were ever going to stick around. Falling for men I barely knew wasn't smart. It wasn't responsible. Especially two of them at the same time.

But whatever excuses the logical part of my brain threw at me, whatever reasons I used to convince myself it wasn't smart to feel anything for them, were shot down by my heart.

They even got along with Lucas, which if they hadn't would have been a huge, rational reason to distance myself from them.

Instead, reliable, smart, always doing the right thing Kandace was warring again with the Kandace that wanted to love life a little more. The me who was finally doing so.

Monday morning, walking into the office was a relief, as I'd always liked this job.

A few years ago, when Andrew sold his internet porn business, he'd asked me to be his financial adviser. I'd worked in an office like that for years, but my job was administrative—I hadn't done things like make investment decisions.

Then again, neither did most of the investors. It was a massive company, and the computers and contracts made most of the decisions about where to put the cash. Andrew said I was a much better choice than any of them, and hired me on the same commission based type of salary those investors had made.

And I was good at what I did, surprising me, but apparently not him. The entire thing led to an invitation to join the partnership here at the Rafael group, where they actually put some thought into the start-ups they supported. The other people here believed in helping good ideas grow and reach their potential, the way I did.

As cheesy as it sounded, every day I saw people's dreams come true, and I loved it.

I settled into my desk for the morning ritual of

beginning work. Checking my calendar to remind myself which meetings I needed to be in. Going through email to decide where the priorities lay—

I frowned at the message from a general contractor whose name I frequently gave to new clients. I'd been considering sending Joystick to him as well, because the contractor was honest and good at his job.

Based on recent events, we're no longer comfortable working with your business partners. I ask that you stop referring people to us immediately.

What the…?

Occasionally we got messages like this, especially if someone we'd sent a vendor's way was a pain in the ass to work with, but as far as I knew we hadn't done any of that lately.

No reason to burn the bridge further. I typed up a quick reply. *I understand. If there's anything I can do to change your mind, please let me know. You've been a great business partner. Wishing you the best.*

I put the message to the back of my mind and moved on, but a nagging thought I couldn't quite grasp lingered.

I had moved on to prepping for my first meeting when a knock drew my attention.

Xander was standing in my office doorway, leaning casually against the frame, looking very much like a man who knew the room would listen to him if he so much as cleared his throat. It was easy to see why some people were drawn to a presence like his, with his salt and pepper hair, hard body, and looming presence. His husband and girlfriend certainly liked it.

I was looking for— *Less flashy* wasn't the right phrase, not when I thought of Joystick. Though Eli definitely had that quiet-but-smart-and-fun-and-sexy…

"What can I do for you?" I wrapped the random and disruptive thoughts up for later.

"Wanted to make sure Lucas got everything taken care of," Xander said.

I nodded. "He's all set. Thank you for rescuing him."

"Anytime." Xander's tone was casual and friendly. "Speaking of all that, you know a lot of people gossip in a place like Haddarville."

I raised my brows, not trying to hide my surprise at the statement. "I know you don't typically care about what they have to say."

"It's true, I don't. But this time I'm hearing whispers that you're spending a lot of time up there."

People cared where I spent my weekends? Why did that bring a flush of heat to my cheeks? I didn't care what they were saying.

But I did care about the reasons I'd been doing exactly that—spending a lot of time in the small town. Especially after this weekend. It seemed like each time I saw Joystick, each time I talked to Eli, the tug to them got stronger, and the resistance got weaker.

The indoctrination was still there, though. The voice saying loving them both was irresponsible.

Inappropriate. Going to hurt the people I would do anything for.

I shook the thoughts aside. "I have been. And?"

"And nothing. Let the fuckers talk, who cares? My only point is, I wouldn't mind letting that house go, if you knew someone who was interested in it."

"You can't just offload your investment properties off on me." I let out a light laugh.

Xander shrugged. "I'm just saying, the offer is there. I'd even sell for market value, and not try to milk you for more."

"Very generous of you."

"Isn't it though?" His grin faded at the sound of a phone chirp, and he grabbed the device from his pocket. A frown sank in as he stared at the screen.

That couldn't be good. "Everything all right?"

He gave a brief shake of his head. "I've got one of our network wiring partners asking me to lose their number."

Twice in one day? "Who'd you piss off?" My teasing didn't come so easily or lightly this time.

"Don't know. I'll catch up with you later." Xander wandered away, still focused on his phone.

Weird. Maybe it was a full moon or something.

I dove into my own work, which occupied my mind for the next few hours. I hit a lull, and my stomach decided to remind me it was after one and all I'd had today was a large coffee. I should go grab something and check my messages while I had a couple of hours where I wasn't expected to be in meetings.

There was a text waiting for me from Daria, from about half an hour ago. *I'm gonna be at Broilers with Brooke in about thirty, if you want to join us.*

I checked the timestamp on the message against my clock. I was only about five minutes late. Grilled sandwiches sounded like a good lunch, and Daria and Brooke's company would be a great way to spend that time.

Seven or eight months ago, before my trip to Milan, I would've preferred the working version of eating. Asked Daria if we could make it a meeting, though Brooke didn't work for or with us.

Today, I just wanted to hang out with my girl-friends.

Hmm.

I sent back a quick note. *Just saw this. On my way.*

As I walked the short distance to the cafe, the sun chased away the chill in the air, and buoyed my mood. By the time I reached my destination, my mind was light, and I was looking forward to the food and the company.

Daria and Brooke waved to me from their table when I walked in, and returned the gesture before heading to the counter. The man who took my order was the owner. He had a beard down to the middle of his chest that he braided, and tied off with intricate beads. His hair was done in a similar style. He called himself The French Viking and he was a hoot.

When I joined Daria and Brooke, they oohed and ahhed over my new hair.

"I love the purple," Daria said.

Brooke studied me. "I wish I had the nerve to do something like that. So pretty."

"You should do it." Who was I? The woman with the *I wish I could* hair, encouraging others to do the same. "I promise, if you love it now, you'll love it even more when it's you." Why was I fighting this Kandace? Why had I ever...?

Brooke twirled a strand of long, dark hair around one finger. "Maybe. I couldn't cut it that short, though. Deacon says this is the perfect pulling length." Her cheeks turned pink. "Not that yours doesn't look incredible at that length. You really look good. Like, happier."

"She's right. You've almost got a glow to you." Daria chimed in. "New project? New car? New guy? What has you in such a great mood?"

"Life." Also, two new guys. "It's a good day. I have good company." The response came easily. I really did feel good, just in a general great mood kind of way.

Their sandwiches arrived, and while I insisted they not wait for me, they insisted they would. A short while later, I had my food as well.

"What brings you to town, Brooke?" I asked as we dug in.

She lived in the same town as Lyndsay. The same place Eli and Joystick were staying.

"Dropping off some scrap for Quentin. He says he's working on something spectacular." Brooke picked stray pieces of bacon from the edge of her sandwich and nibbled.

"Ooh, I'm excited to see it." I liked his work. He was a metal worker and sculptor who had a couple of pieces in prominent spots around the valley, thanks to Carly getting his talent in front of the right people. His art was always unique and breathtaking. "Any hints about what it is?"

Brooke shook her head. "I didn't ask. I wanted to be surprised. There were a couple of vintage bike rims in the mix, and three rusted watering tins. The rest was scrap metal."

"She said, glossing over the fact that there was at least one wooden dildo in there." Daria tossed the comment out as if it were the most casual reply she could make.

"I don't think I want to consider the infection implications of wood..." I pointed a look between my legs, "... down there. Besides, aren't there splinters?"

Brooke's blush was back. "I assure you, they're highly polished."

"Highly polished and *very* well worn." Daria's tone was playful.

This was both entertaining and embarrassing. A year ago, I never would've had this conversation with other people, or even considered the topic. Especially in public. Especially with a woman who worked for me.

But one drunken night, I'd told Carly I wished I had friends. What a silly thing to say, but it was true. I'd spent so much time working, doing what was *proper* that I'd never really gotten close to anyone. In any way, not just romantic.

Carly made sure I was *one of the girls* after that.

Had I been changing longer than I wanted to admit? This was a good thing, wasn't it?

"So, are we going to talk about the elephant in the room?" Daria's tone shifted in a blink.

This was about Joystick. I wasn't sure why I was so certain, but I was. "Is there an elephant?"

"I got a call from a tile contractor today, someone Carly put Joystick in touch with, and the guy is severing ties," Daria said. "When I went into the system to mark his name, I found at least three more contacts deactivated today."

"Yeah. I don't know what's going on." But I did. The moment the words left my mouth the pieces clicked. "Unless it was... Fuck."

"Your name in that smear piece that went viral this weekend." Daria's voice was kind rather than accusatory. "Probably not my place to say, but fuck those guys. Why do they care whether or not we're associated with some random former child star, when so many start-ups out there are run by megalomaniacal assholes?"

"She's got a point," Brooke said.

Daria did have a point, but the entire situation sank in and weighed on my mind. If this was really related to the news about Joystick, to my connection to him…

I didn't put any of the blame on him, but if our agency was suffering because I'd hooked up with him…

There were so many bits of my job that I loved, but one of the things I could leave behind forever was that sometimes people who didn't do anything wrong got hurt. Sometimes assholes got their way, and unpleasant steps had to be taken to fix things, even if those steps weren't fair.

I didn't want to think about what a *not fair* solution would be in this case, but a little whisper was in my head anyway, chanting about how I was losing Joystick.

25
joystick

THIS WEEKEND WAS INCREDIBLE. I wanted a billion more like it.

Maybe not *just* like it—it would be great when I could walk again. Kandace and Eli and I could do so much more. More exploring. More playing. More living.

I hated that the bad press was stressing them both out. There wasn't really a good way to tell someone *it'll pass, and people will forget in a few days* until they'd lived the experience at least once or twice themselves.

But it *would* pass, and we'd all still be here. I needed to make sure Eli and Kandace stuck around. I needed them to know I needed them.

My brain had run out of words, apparently.

Because I was bored out of my mind sitting around this house all day with nothing to do but think. I couldn't make much more headway on my restaurant from here, and I could only do so much massive grand gesture planning from the couch.

That was my next important task—figure out how to tell Eli I loved him. How to make sure Kandace knew she had to be a part of our lives.

And I wanted to let each of them know in such a way that no movie or TV show confession would ever hold a candle to when I told them how much they meant to me.

I sent Kandace a text asking her to call me back when she had a free moment. Eli would be home tonight so I'd tell him then. We'd talk about next steps. I'd make sure that when my ankle was healed, he didn't leave.

My brain needed to chew on the details of how I would accomplish all that though. A change of scenery was in order, so I would start with getting a cab or an Uber or something, to chauffeur me around town for a few hours.

Carly's face flashed on my phone screen, and I answered. "Yellow."

"Does Kandace know you have another woman's fingerprints all over your social media?" She greeted me. She must be talking about the apologies Lyndsay helped me draft.

I grinned. Carly was all business until she wasn't —something she had in common with Kandace, though Kandace wore it better.

And yes, I was very biased. "Kandace introduced us. Is it that obvious I didn't write the posts myself?"

"You're not really an *apologize for things* kind of guy."

I'd be apologizing to Eli until the end of time if that was what it took to keep him. "I am when I'm wrong."

"How often are you wrong?"

"Hard to say, but you've never seen it."

Carly laughed. "My point exactly. Look, I just called to offer my sympathy, and send Raul and Diego's as well. I'm sorry Isabella is doing this to you."

"Eh. Bad press comes with the territory. But I do worry about how it's impacting everyone else."

"That's the other reason I called." Seriousness replaced the teasing in Carly's voice. "Don't let Kandace walk away over this."

It was good to have friends in the right places, and Carly was one of the most loyal. If she was on my side, I definitely had a shot with Kandace. "The last thing I want is to lose her. Tell me how to win her over."

"No." Carly's flat refusal caught me off-guard.

"Isn't that why you called though? You don't want to see your favorite brother in law happy forever and ever?" Okay, so neither Raul or Diego was actually my family, but they'd become good friends while I was there, and I'd joked a few times about us being long-lost brothers.

"I don't pick favorites," Carly said. "But I promise you he's already happy forever and ever."

"You're my favorite sister-in-law." I didn't think the flattery would work on her, but I had to try.

"You're an only child." Her eye roll was practically audible. "But Diego and Raul appreciate the sentiment. I'm not going to tell you how to win Kandace over because she already loves me, and you need her to feel that way about *you*. Besides, she'll recognize my influence as well as I did Lyndsay's on your BikBok."

"Fair point." Not that I was conceding I was wrong, only that Carly was right.

"What are you going to do?"

I had no idea. "You don't want to help, so you don't get to know until it happens."

"Asshole." Teasing-Carly was back.

"Yup. Give Eloise a kiss for me and I expect to see all of you out here for my Grand Opening," I said.

"*I* expect to see details to said event sooner rather than later."

I hoped so. "Cross my heart. Talk soon."

That was what I'd do with my day—inspiration struck as I hung up. I'd check out that location Eli and Kandace mentioned would be good for a restaurant. This wasn't a prime location, but my research said it was growing, and right now the town really only had pizza and burgers. It could use a third choice.

The next problem was, there was no local cab company, and none of the driver apps showed anyone available in my area. How was I supposed to get to Main Street?

A quick search online brought back a phone number for Johnny's Garage, and a moment later I was dialing and asking to speak with Cash.

I introduced myself as a friend of Lyndsay's—the brief exchange between him and her on Saturday told me that was my in. "Do you maybe know where a guy in a leg cast can get a ride in this town?" I asked.

"If you're not picky about the way said ride looks, I'd be happy to haul you around in my pickup for a couple of hours."

Not at all what I expected. "Don't you need to work? You make that offer to a lot of people?"

"Things are slow right now, and they'll call me in if they need me. Besides, Lyndsay told me what you're dealing with. It sucks. Plus she spoke highly of you, so you can't be that bad a guy."

"I'm a *great* guy."

Cash chuckled. "I'll be by in a few."

I had him drop me at Gage's where I spent half an hour or so discussing distribution possibilities. In other words, what would it take for me to sell his beer at my new place if I were to open up down the street.

We reached what seemed like a great agreement for both of us. He offered to drive me to my next destination. Were all the people here so nice? I loved it. I told him it wasn't far, and I really needed to move after being cooped up for so long inside.

I got that some people loved home, but I needed to see people. To meet new people. I had my crutches, and I hobbled across the street to an honest-to-God record store, with an empty-but-recently-remodeled shop space next to it.

This must be the place. The music shop was incredible inside. Records and CDs were framed with signed pictures of the artist, and decorated the walls. There were rows with all different mediums, from vinyl to 8-track, to micro discs, and the music playing over the speakers was classic Depeche Mode.

"Let me know if I can help you find anything." The man behind the counter wore a faded black T-shirt that matched the music, and ripped jeans. He was probably a few years older than me.

I liked him already. "You can help me find Onyx."

"That's me. What can I do you for?"

"I understand the property next door, the one that's for sale, is yours."

His expression flickered, and pleasant became a frown for a heartbeat before his face returned to normal. "It is. You probably get this a lot, but you look a lot like that kid from that TV show, Donovan? What was his name, Austin? I mean, you look *just* like him, all the way down to the tattoos he picked up when he gave up the child star life."

I had a feeling he knew he was talking about me, and I couldn't hide my grin at being recognized. "Joystick, not Austin. And I didn't give it up, I grew up. Did you *give up* high school life?"

"Before I ever started. Turns out John Hughes lied about how much appeal the quiet, nerdy kid held for the big star quarterback."

Yeah, TV got a lot of things wrong about real life. "Do you even have a high school football team here?"

Onyx cocked his head and studied me, any hint of teasing vanishing. Not that there had been much. "What makes you think I'm from *here*?"

"It's not the kind of town people move *into*."

Onyx shrugged. "You did. Gossip says that *big movie star* Donovan came to town with the indie film caravan."

He had me there. "Tell me about the space next door."

"It was a diner attached to the record store, decades ago. It was already closed when I took this place over, and I wasn't interested in running both, so I left it closed."

Simple enough. "What do you picture there?" I drifted in the direction of what looked like a door dividing the two spaces.

Onyx pulled a set of keys from his pocket and flipped through them until he stopped on one that looked like all the others to my eye. "Wouldn't be my call, because it wouldn't be my space." He unlocked the door.

"But you have a vision. You remodeled recently."

One corner of Onyx's mouth tugged up. "I've got a lot of visions, but I'm not Reese Witherspoon now any more than I was Judd Nelson in high school."

My brain stalled. "Why Reese Witherspoon?"

"We could also go with Sandra Bullock or Meg Ryan if you prefer." Onyx pushed into the available space. "Most likely actresses to own fictional small-town businesses that are bought up by men from the city with more money and sex appeal than brains, but in the end, through lots of humor and a few sighs, I'd win his heart and the business would stay mine."

I liked this guy. It wasn't often I got to meet someone whose references were so on-point. What did his big city guy look like? "What if the person who bought this restaurant space wanted to fill it with things like movie trivia night and other fandoms?" That was my vision anyway, but he'd understand it better than most.

Onyx finally cracked a smile. "I like it. Would you like the grand tour?" He glanced at my cast. "Or the abbreviated version?

"Most definitely."

We spent the next hour or so bouncing between tangents and details about the available property. As suspected, he'd recently remodeled the space, including brand new ovens, fridge, all the basics I needed for a restaurant.

I couldn't buy the first place I saw, especially out here in the middle of nowhere, regardless of how loudly my heart said this was the place to grab. But he was happy to rent it to me for the evening, to get a feel for how I liked it.

"You going to be okay, hobbling around on that?" He nodded at my cast.

As long as no one told my doctor, I'd be fine. "I've got it."

I couldn't stay on my feet as long as I wanted, but that just meant taking frequent breaks. The downtime was perfect for calling anyone I'd met locally to buy supplies, and the rest of the time was for cooking. Prepping for dinner tonight.

And when I was close to ready, I texted Eli and asked him to meet me here.

His reply said, *what are you... Never mind. I'll be there.*

About fifteen minutes later, I was letting him into the restaurant that had a single table decorated with a tablecloth, and settings for two.

The instant I locked the door behind him, he whirled on me. "What the hell are you doing? How long did you spend down here? You can't be on your feet. We talked about this."

Aww. He cared.

I knew he did.

"Well?" Eli looked at me expectantly.

My answer was to press my mouth to his and kiss him for everything I was worth.

26
elijah

I SPENT the day arguing with Andrew about rewrites. Not because we actually disagreed, but he was that stressed out. I'd never seen him like this, and didn't think it was possible.

Not that I blamed him when he finally admitted he'd lost another investor in the film.

"Not sure why they care about Joystick's bad press given your past and what your movie is about," I tried to keep my tone light.

Andrew almost cracked a smile.

"I mean, you're a former fucking porn king," I said. "Making this movie, with the stars you have, is already one huge *fuck the world.*"

Andrew grinned. "I like the way you think."

The rest of the work day went smoother, until Austin messaged me and asked me to meet him on Main Street. I was torn between concern and fury.

Why was he there? Was he hurt? Was he being impulsive again and risking getting hurt?

I knocked on the door to the vacant restaurant ready to take him to a clinic if needed and scold him if not.

When he kissed me, I forgot it all. Nothing mattered except the way his mouth molded to mine, and the grip of his fingers digging into my arms. His lips, soft but also hard and demanding.

Yeah, we'd kissed a few times recently, but this was different. There was a power in this. An intensity I couldn't ignore.

A kind of promise I'd spent a long time convincing myself that I'd never have from Austin.

When we broke apart, I couldn't find my voice or my thoughts. I needed to cling to him so I wouldn't float away.

"I'm sorry." Austin's words fell over my cheek as he kissed along my jaw. "For anything in the past that kept us apart. That you hurt for so long. But I'm not sorry for this."

I didn't… "What is *this*?"

"Dinner."

As if a single word answer would provide any answers about what we were doing here. "Away from the house. Lights dimmed. Only one table…"

"This is the part of the story where I woo you." Austin made his answer sound like it was the only logical one.

I was tired of fighting what I felt for him. "You've

already wooed me." I'd had so much fun since I ran into him again. Since I met Kandace. Since the three of us came together. "I don't blame you for what happened back then, when we were separated. I'm tired of holding onto the bitterness. I want my friend back."

Austin drew his thumb along my bottom lip, sending shivers down my spine. "Just friends?" He asked.

"No. Our friendship has always been at the core of who we are. Without that, I wouldn't want more."

"You do then. Want more? Because I do. I don't want you to go away again. I want you by my side, wherever that is, and I love you so much it makes my heart sing and *God damn it*, I need you Elijah. So, so much."

And then Austin was kissing me again. Drawing the connection out. Filling my mind with a million racing thoughts this time instead of clearing my head.

An acrid scent greeted me, and I broke away to sniff. "Is that smoke?"

"Because we're so hot together?" Austin teased.

"Because you left something on the stove that you shouldn't have?"

Austin scrambled to grab his crutches, but our kissing had taken us away from them. "Fuck, fuck, fuck."

I grabbed the nearest chair, pushed it behind him, and made him sit. "Stay here." I walked toward the kitchen before he could protest or stop me.

When I reached the back, I found a series of plates and dishes set up, as if he was just waiting to do the last steps of cooking. He'd really gone all out for this, and as much as I wanted to be upset with him for moving around when he should be keeping his weight off his foot, I was also touched.

I found the offending liquid—or what had once been liquid—on the stove in a saucepan. It was dark red and lumpy and would never see good days again. I turned off the heat and moved the pan to a cold burner, then took the pause to clear my head.

This should be the moment where I paused and considered what I was getting myself into, but there was nothing to think about. I wanted this and him, and the only caveat was one I was pretty sure he felt the same way about—I wanted Kandace to be a part of it too.

I returned to the dining room to find Austin sitting where I'd left him, wearing a pout.

"What's the look for?" I asked. "Is that because I made you sit?"

"It's because you didn't answer my question. Do you want more?"

"I might have answered if someone—" I shot him a pointed look—"hadn't stuck his tongue down my throat."

Austin grinned. "Worth it."

Though I knew exactly what to say, it wouldn't hurt to drag this out just a little. "I think the… blood? Is ruined." I nodded toward the kitchen.

"Berry compote," he corrected me. "For dessert."

"Wow." I really was impressed. There were so many layers to this man...

"You're killing me," Austin said.

Teasing time was over. I crouched in front of him so I could look him in the eye. "You didn't have to do all of this."

"I did, or I wouldn't be me." He had a point. "Answer my question."

I brushed my lips over his. "Yes, I want more from you. From us. I never got over you, and I think that's why it hurt so much to see you again, happy and friendly, as if I'd never happened."

"No." Austin shook his head. "I was so happy when I saw you again, at the side of the road, because it was like we were getting a second chance at something that might have just been a childhood crush, but was so much more. *Is* so much more."

"There's a *but* in there." I heard the catch in his voice, and felt it in my mind.

He snickered. "Butt."

"You're such a child." I didn't mean that in a bad way.

"And you love it."

"I do."

"The *but* is Kandace," Austin said.

There she was. Like I expected. Like I hoped. Just her name made my heart flutter. Then again, so did Austin's. I loved him, but what I'd found with her... I couldn't ignore that either. I couldn't give that up.

"I wouldn't want to do this without her. I wouldn't want you to do this without her, whatever *this* becomes." Austin's words echoed my thoughts perfectly.

"So we'll tell her as well."

"Yes." He yanked me closer for another kiss. "But tonight is about you and me."

I leaned into him, tasting his lips. Devouring the low groans he made and feeling them mingle with mine. This felt incredible—in my heart and my mind. And *God* the way he kissed.

"I love you, Joystick." The name tasted odd on my tongue, but his kisses chased the strangeness away. Besides, if that was what he preferred, I could make the switch. Of all the things that required compromise, *Joystick* was a pretty simple one, and really making this all work meant the world to me. He and Kandace meant the world to me.

27
kandace

I WAS EXHAUSTED when I got home from work. Not in a bad way; some days required a lot of mental power, but that meant I'd gotten to solve problems and learn new things.

The last thing I wanted to be thinking about were the severed ties with vendors and contractors, or how it may be indirectly my fault, but the notion was there with no brain filters to stop it.

I had enough sense to realize this entire mess was Isabella's doing, not mine. I'd love to give that woman a piece of my mind if I ever met her again. The fallout impacted me regardless, though. Me and those around me. If this was what happened when bad press hit, and I were to stay with Joystick, would we deal with this every time someone spread bad gossip about him?

I could probably learn to take it, but the firm...

I was too drained to think about it tonight. Making

decisions at times like these was never a good idea. Stripping off my shoes, my belt, and my bra, I collapsed onto the couch in a grateful heap. After taking a few minutes to be a pile of brainless goo, I made myself move. Check the phone messages I'd ignored throughout the day.

Lucas would send me a priority message if he had an emergency, but otherwise he was fine with waiting, and not many others held that kind of priority to me.

Except that I had a text from Joystick, *call me when you get a chance*.

I kind of hated that I'd missed that earlier.

There was a voicemail as well. Eli and Joystick talking over each other, and really only managing to say, *you need to call us* again.

The next message was from Lucas. "Hey. Didn't get the part in Phantom. Mr. Allman said I may want to clean up my public image if I want to work in theater. No clue what that meant. Gonna spend the night with Ben and Jerry. Love you."

The hurt in his voice made me frown. I tried to call him back, but got his voicemail. "Wallowing and no fun. Call me tomorrow."

Poor kid. I sent him a text instead telling him I was here if he needed. I'd seen him go through the theater highs and lows enough that as much as I wanted to wrap him up in a warm mom-hug and tell him everything would be all right, I also knew he would process in his own way.

As I went to call Joystick and Eli back, Lucas's message bounced in my thoughts. *Clean up my public image.*

Lucas didn't have a bad public image. He was a Straight A college student who loved musicals and football games.

What did that mean?

I wasn't going to be the mom who interfered in her kid's school business—not something like this—but the words taunted me.

This didn't have anything to do with me, did it?

It couldn't.

The thought didn't leave me that night, though. And the next morning I still couldn't figure out what kind of bad public image Lucas might have that would keep him out of a college musical. Was I missing something about his behavior? Was I living in denial about how my son spent his free time?

It didn't seem likely, but I couldn't get rid of the thought. I needed to know.

I checked out Dr. Allman's office hours to make sure I could catch him, told work I'd be in a little late, and headed to the university. I wasn't going to be the mom who yelled at a teacher for things that weren't their fault. I wouldn't demand Lucas be given a role he hadn't earned.

But if something was happening with him and I'd missed it...

I didn't want to be that mother either.

A short while later I was shaking Dr. Allman's hand and we were exchanging pleasantries.

"What can I do for you, Ms. Newton?" He asked.

I wanted to approach this delicately, rather than unhinged. "I'd like to talk to you about what you said to Lucas yesterday."

Like that, the professor's expression shifted to stony. "What about it?"

"You said something about his public image."

"That's correct."

What was I supposed to do with a flat response like that? "So it's not about his acting or singing."

"No. In fact he excels at what he does, and if he overcomes his other issues, I did invite him to try out again next year."

I knew my son was good, but it was nice to have the bias confirmed. "What other issues? Forgive me, I'm trying to track down what's actually going on. Is this a matter of grades? Is he struggling someplace else?"

"No."

This wasn't helpful in any way. "I'm not here to tell you how to do your job, Dr. Allman, I'm simply concerned about my son. Can you tell me if it wasn't talent, and it wasn't anything he's done, why he didn't make the list? If there are that many talented students here, then that's fantastic."

The professor's smile was unpleasant. "These productions mean everything to the students who are cast. For many of them it's the start of a career, and for others they simply want to stretch their wings. Every student I chose will pour their hearts and souls into their parts, if they're lucky. The costume makers and set designers will do the same. None of them deserves to have their productions canceled because of bad press about one person."

"You just told me Lucas's reputation wasn't an issue."

"No. But his mother is dating a man responsible for a little girl's kidnapping in another country. You don't think that shit trickles down?"

What? My confusion switched to fury in a blink. Lucas was being denied the part because of *what*? This required a whole new approach. "Let's break your logic down, shall we?" I adopted a cool tone to match Dr. Allman's, and let a professional side of me slide in that I usually reserved for difficult work negotiations. "Who I choose to date is not a reflection of the people around me." No, that wasn't quite right. I hated that the statement wasn't more true. "My son does not pick and choose my boyfriends." Again, not quite true. Not that he gave me permission, but I wouldn't be with someone who Lucas didn't like or who didn't like him. I wasn't doing a great job of this so far.

Time to back up. "Austin wasn't responsible for a kidnapping, and even the article didn't say that, which means you're getting your news from people misinterpreting what they read, instead of reading the source yourself." A fact. That was a good start. "He wasn't involved in any way except helping to find the missing child. If you'd cared to read past the headlines, you'd know this entire thing was the product of a bitter woman looking to blame everyone but herself." Which I needed to avoid in this case. "As for the other students in your production, I pity each and every one of them, that they've chosen to work with you."

"Really. Why is that?" The professor sneered.

"For those who choose to stay in the industry, to work in any public facing job, if they don't already know, they'll learn soon enough that bad publicity and false rumors come with the territory. That's not fair to them, but it's the way the world works. For them to discover at this point in their careers that one of the people who's supposed to support them, that you as their supposed mentor, are more worried about your own tiny little ego, than you are about your students... That will crush a lot of them.

"If any of them stops to think for a moment about the fact that you would rather throw a mentee under the bus, that you would rather cave to fear-mongering and gossip, than stand by someone who's being slandered... The only thing some of them will take from this experience is that the people who are supposed to support them can't be trusted any more than anyone else. And that's a horrible lesson to be responsible for teaching another human being."

"I don't—"

I silenced him with a glare. "I'll recommend to

Lucas that he consider a different path—community theater, another school, whatever keeps him away from you—for him to pursue this dream. But *I* understand that sometimes we have to associate with unpleasant people, and that's not an individual's fault. You have a good day, Dr. Allman."

I stalked from the office, ignoring any of his stammering. Rage spilled through me still, making me feel like I'd drunk two pots of coffee brewed with energy drinks.

Despite what I'd told Dr. Allman, I didn't want my decisions to have this kind of impact on Lucas. Could I really be with Joystick and Eli if this was what it was going to do to my family?

28
joystick

WHEN KANDACE DIDN'T GET BACK to Eli or me on Monday, I was bummed, but I figured life happened.

Neither of us heard from her on Tuesday either, and that worried me. I called and went straight to voicemail, so I left a message saying we missed her, and hoped she was all right.

There was still no answer.

In between all of that, I didn't just sit around and wait for Kandace, though I thought of her in every free minute, and during lots of the busy ones as well. When Eli was home, we had so much fun together. There was still tension, still some unfamiliarity about who we were then versus now, but the biggest obstacle between us, the resentment of the last fifteen years, was gone.

Eli was so smart. Sarcastic. Entertaining.

I loved everything about having him back in my life.

He checked with Andrew, to make sure Kandace was all right. Andrew's response was basically that she was fine, but if she hadn't told us herself why she wasn't talking to us, she had a reason and he respected that.

Which I understood, but only as the logic applied to anyone who wasn't me or Eli.

Thursday night I sent her another text. *Hope to see you Friday night. If you're busy, we'll come down there and have dinner with you.*

Friday, early afternoon, the doorbell rang. *Kandace* was the first and only name that popped into my head. "Are you here to rob me or take advantage of me?" I called out playfully, as I grabbed my crutches and hobbled to the door. Lucas was on the other side. "Oh."

"Nice to see you too. Sorry I'm not my mom." His smile was dry. "Does asking that work for you?"

I stepped aside to let him in, and headed back to the couch. "I have yet to be robbed or taken advantage of, so I'm going to say yes."

"Has anyone visited who you don't know?" Lucas asked.

"The kid who delivered my lunch the other day."

"Lyndsay's son. He wasn't here to do either of those things."

True, but this was a fun conversation. "Are you certain?"

Lucas snorted. "I've known him since she joined the firm a few years ago. I'm pretty certain, yeah."

"It's always the quiet ones." I pushed the warning tone into my voice along with a dramatic flair.

"Thank God we're both safe." Lucas took a seat across from me and set a book on the coffee table. "This is the restaurant supplier list Mom promised you last weekend. She said she couldn't find a digital copy."

Like that, the fun mood was gone. If he was bringing me the book...

"She tried to get Lyndsay to drop it off for you, but I intercepted," Lucas said.

... It meant she was avoiding me and or Eli for some unknown reason. Not that I hadn't already figured that out. "Why isn't she bringing it herself?"

"She's..." Lucas sighed and seemed to deflate in his seat. "If you like her, you have to do something."

I needed more information first. "She's what? Do I need to apologize? I'll do anything." I didn't care if I sounded desperate—I was.

"I don't want to tell you because I don't want to hurt your feelings." Lucas chewed on his bottom lip.

I didn't even fucking care. "Tell me."

"She's worried that if she sees more of you and Eli, that it'll hurt me."

What? "She knows you love us, right?"

A brief grin flashed across Lucas's face. "Random dudes on the street know I love you guys. But..." He grabbed the book again and dragged his thumb along the corner of the spine. "I shouldn't tell you this, but I'm going to because I trust you. Not because you were on TV, but because I've never seen Mom as happy as she has been the last few weeks."

We were getting serious now. "I cross my heart, whatever you say here is as sacred and secret as you tell me that it needs to be."

As I said that, Eli walked into the house.

"What's going on?" he asked.

"Lucas is going to help us figure out how to talk to Kandace." I hoped that was right.

Lucas looked between us both. "Okay, so you didn't hear this from me, except that I will tell her I told you but... Mom was raised in an interesting household. We'll call her parents Grandma and Grandpa, but they never were to me. Grandpa insisted his kids be brought up Catholic. Educated Catholic. Live and breathe and die Catholic. He worked hard—too hard—and adored Grandma. He never told her no. She spent a lot of time doing what-ever struck her fancy. Partying. Spending a few months at a time working on her college degree before dropping out. Starting random businesses…

"Those all sound like great things, except to Grandma, Mom was an obstacle that got in the way of having fun. Mom basically raised herself until Andrew came along. She won't tell the story this way, but he knows what he was born into. He was Grand-pa's son, and basically became their only child. Mom raised him, too, because Grandma was too busy. When eighteen hit, Mom split as fast as she could."

"Don't blame her," Eli muttered. The anger

splashed across his face matched what boiled inside me.

"I think she felt bad about abandoning Andrew. He has a lot of Grandma in him, but he's not oblivious. I think he realized that Mom—Kandace—was the glue keeping that family together. Even though she'd gotten her own place, he spent a lot more time with her than at home. She let him. He was just a kid and none of this was his fault."

The more of this story I heard, the more my fury rose. How could anyone do that to their child, their children? Kandace deserved so much more than that. This made me love her more, too. Maybe that was the wrong reaction, but hearing about the kind of strength she had showed me she really was the woman I thought she was. Kind. Resilient. Incredible.

"Andrew told me all of this because he hates that they—their parents—stole Kandace's life. She's going to keep her distance from the two of you because she doesn't want any of this to hurt me. Because she only knows how to look out for other people, not herself. I promise I'll be fine, but you need to tell her how you feel," Lucas said.

The expression on Eli's face matched my turmoil. My anger and sadness. "We can't tell her anything if she won't talk to us," he said.

"I think you need to tell her how you feel." If one thing would get Kandace's attention, it would be her son saying hey, mom, listen up. "I—we—will sweep her off her feet if she lets us, but Lucas, you have to tell her she needs to start living for her."

Lucas's brows bunched up and he twisted his mouth. "I guess I do."

"You haven't done that yet?" Eli sounded surprised.

"We're close and all, but I don't want to hurt her, either. I still need her, you know? She's my mom. But I also want her to do good things for her."

Another thing I adored about them was how close Kandace was with Lucas. I also knew, "You're the center of her universe. If anyone can make her listen, make her understand, it's going to be you," I said. "She raised you to be independent. To be strong." I couldn't guarantee that, but it seemed pretty clear from his actions. "This isn't you telling her you don't need her. This is just the next step in growing up."

"Yeah, I guess so." Lucas let out a light huff. "Can you travel with that thing?" He nodded at my cast.

"No," Eli said.

Bullshit I couldn't. "Yes."

"Then be at Mom's tomorrow a little after eleven in the morning. I'm making her brunch. I'll tell her it's important that if she likes you both, she needs to be with you, and then you can have her for the rest of the weekend." Lucas paused with a frown. "Eww, me. Phrasing."

I chuckled, but let the sound fade quickly. This was serious. "We'll be there. Won't we?" I looked at Eli.

He nodded. "Wouldn't miss it for the world."

Lucas wrote down the address for us, and we just had to pray that Kandace would hear us out.

29

kandace

I MISSED Eli and Joystick so much that the feeling was a constant ache in my heart. I hadn't called them back because I needed to break things off with them, but hadn't found the strength to do so.

I worked late on Friday night, to keep my mind off the fact I was spending it by myself. When my phone rang a little after seven, and *Jonathan* flashed on the screen, I wasn't surprised. He was one of the partners based out of California, and he always put in long nights when his wife was out of the country on buying trips for her art gallery.

"Hey," I answered, grateful for the distraction.

"Oh. Hey." He sounded surprised. "I didn't expect you to pick up."

"Then why'd you call?"

"So I didn't forget before Monday."

That made sense. I'd always liked Jonathan. I liked most of the partners, but he was one of the founders, and his approach to business had always clicked with mine. "What can I do for you?"

"Since I have you, instead of your voicemail, how are you holding up with everything?" he asked.

It sucked. I wanted it all and couldn't have it. Why couldn't I just reach out and grab something for myself for once? "I'm all right. Worried about what the bad press is doing to the firm."

His chuckle surprised me. "Don't. Don't put any kind of thought into it."

"Why not?" I expected an answer like that from Xander, but not Jonathan.

"We deal with bad press all the time, you know that. The incident with Aaron was far worse than this."

That was pretty bad. "Still. We're losing vendors. People are talking."

"Some contacts spook easily. We always recover. They tend to come back when they realize the cost of walking away, and if they don't, we find new ones. You know how this works."

I was familiar with what he was talking about. "It's different when I'm the one at fault."

"This isn't your fault." His assurance came without hesitation. "If this were happening to one of the other partners, how would you react?"

I hadn't thought of it that way. I should've, but I'd gotten too caught up in the bad. "Sometimes things get blown out of proportion, but we're all good at what we do. Fine, I see your point."

"We've got this. *You've* got this."

My smile came without my permission. "Thank you. So why did you really call?"

"Can you put me in touch with Andrew?"

"My brother?"

The men had spoken a couple of times in the past. They had a few mutual friends, but as far as I was aware, Andrew and Jonathan were just a little too different to enjoy each other's company long-term.

"That's the one," Jonathan said.

I shrugged at my empty office. "Sure. Can I ask why?"

"This movie of his, with this kind of publicity? It's about to blow up in a big way. I want in." Jonathan had an instinct for reading how the money was going to follow high-profile situations. It was how he'd made his money when he was younger, and that gut feeling still served him well.

If he thought this was the kind of chatter that would turn out to be good, it was hard to argue that.

"Of course." I gave him Andrew's number, and we said our *goodnights*.

The conversation lingered in my head long after I hung up, though. There was something there I needed to see and I couldn't quite grasp it.

SPENDING SATURDAY MORNING with Lucas was a nice distraction though. He'd offered to come over and

Allyson Lindt

make brunch. He hadn't mentioned the guys at all, which was odd, but I was grateful for it.

It would be nice if I could stop thinking about them at all. If Joystick opened a restaurant here, would there ever be a point where I could look him in the eye again? The obvious answer was yes because I always did what I needed to, but I wouldn't like doing so, if I walked away from him and Eli.

Not *if* but *when*. There was no way we could all be together. I needed to get rid of any notion of that.

I tried instead to focus on Lucas catching me up on his week while we ate. Dr. Allman had offered him an understudy role in the musical, and he turned it down. He said *because you're right, Mom. He doesn't deserve me*.

I had such a great kid. Not only that he was strong enough to make that decision with that kind of confidence, but also that he could carry this conversation, because I sure as hell wasn't giving him the attention he deserved.

"What about you?" He turned to me as we were finishing up the meal.

"What about me?" I gathered a stack of dishes and carried them to the sink.

He followed. "I've talked this entire time about me. How are you? How was your week? How are you not going nuts being with your men?"

I tripped on the air, and my heart caught in my throat. "I'm fine."

"You miss them." Lucas took the plates and

glasses from me, rinsed them, and put them in the dishwasher.

I should've known we wouldn't make it through the whole meal without this coming up. Best to squash the topic now. "Sometimes we have to make sacrifices—"

"No." Lucas cut me off.

"Excuse me?"

"I mean, yes, sometimes we all make sacrifices, but this is not one of those times."

If only that were true. I returned to the dining room table to wipe it down. "It is."

Lucas stepped between me and the table. "Your entire life, you've done things for everyone else. For me. For Andrew. For your own fucking parents. You always take the smaller slice of cake, and always go without if there's not enough to go around. Do you think I don't see that? Sometimes, it's okay to do things for you."

I was touched that he'd noticed, but that just meant I'd raised a considerate human being, not that I was wrong about this subject. "This is not a thing I can do just for me."

"Because of me? If that's what's holding you back, I hate it. If I'm what's standing in your way, I free you of that obligation."

If only it were that easy. "You. The partners. The firm..." I could go on all day about the people who would be hurt by my actions, every time there was bad press about Joystick.

"I guarantee you, at least some of your business partners have been through similar things. I read the industry blog—gossip is everywhere. They'll have your back on this."

"I can't—"

"Can't what?" Lucas talked over me. "Can't be happy? You need to be. You deserve to be. You're not just the best mom in the world, you're probably one of the best people in the world. You've got a lifetime of karma saved up, and this is your chance to cash a little of it in."

I wanted to argue. I also wanted what he was saying to be real. I wanted the latter so much.

Lucas threw his arms around me in a tight hug, startling me. "I love you, Mom. I love everything you've done for me, and everything you've given me. It's time to live for you. Even if I have to make you do so for me."

I laughed at his faulty-but-sweet logic. "Not sure it works that way."

"It does if that's what it takes."

The doorbell rang.

"Fuck, they're early," Lucas muttered.

My gut twisted. "Who is?"

He stepped back and looked me in the eye. "Please, Mom. If you don't like them then walk away, but don't do it for any reason besides that. No arguments. You know I'm right."

I wasn't convinced, but I also didn't have an argument. "I'll hear them out." Damn it, I did want this. I did want Joystick and Eli.

The bell chimed again, followed by a knock.

Lucas grinned and practically skipped to answer.

Joystick and Eli would be on the other side. The butterflies in my gut knew it before Lucas opened the door. My heart fluttered. Excitement surged despite my trying to squash it. I shouldn't be so excited to see them again, but I was.

"Is your mother home?" Isabella's voice curdled my insides.

Fury replaced my doubt. What I wanted wasn't unreasonable—Love. To be loved. To do more than just exist or survive.

And this woman, this creature who abandoned her child, who chose to blame everyone but herself for her problems, and who reminded me too much of my own mother, thought she was owed the world because she pouted and fluttered her eyelashes and stomped her feet.

I composed myself and went to the door. Seeing her, my brain stalled. She was dressed in a T-shirt and jeans, but she looked immaculate. Straight off the cover of a fashion magazine. Her make-up was on point and there wasn't a single strand of hair out of place. How was that possible with a messy bun?

On the other hand I was in yoga pants, my shirt had paint stains on it, and I wore the same basic pony-tail I'd pulled my hair into when I got up this morning.

I could stand here and feel inadequate, or I could remember the woman in front of me had hurt so many people I cared about, and it was unlikely she gave a shit about any of those consequences. Who the fuck cared how good she looked?

"Hi, Hon. I got your information from your brother. Do you have a minute?" Isabella's voice was fake sugar and syrup.

There was no way Andrew told her where I lived. Did she steal it off his desk? I could withdraw from the fakeness, maybe counter it with my own, but I was done being polite. "As a matter of fact, I don't. Not for you."

"I beg your pardon?" Isabella's mask faded in a blink.

I returned the same phony smile she'd given me both times we met. "I believe you heard me the first time. I don't have a minute for you. You're a myopic, narcissistic creature who seems to delight in the attention of others, no matter how good or bad, regardless of how it hurts anyone, and I will not feed that craving in you." I started to swing the door shut.

"I-came-to-apologize." Isabella's run-together words made me pause. "I just needed Joystick to know he'd hurt me. This was never about you."

"No, because it was only ever about you. You like living alone in your own little Isabella world, where you're the queen and everyone else bows to your whims as you spit on them from your glass tower? I'm done wasting words on you, because you're not worth it." This time I let the door swing shut despite the string of protests that faded to her calling me fat old cow, right before I closed my house off from her.

I leaned against the heavy object between me and her, listening to her ring the bell. Hammer on with her fist. Shout another string of obscenities—this time in Italian—and I took one deep breath after another to try to calm myself.

It wasn't working.

Lucas stared at me with wide eyes. What was he thinking?

The noise Isabella was making stopped.

Adrenaline coursed through my veins regardless. Did I really just...? I should feel bad, right? I was waiting for that guilt.

It wasn't there. I'd been justified in telling her what I did. In shutting her out of our lives that way.

Lucas threw his arms around my neck. "You are the coolest mom ever. Holy shit. That was amazing. You cut her down like a Japanese sword, but with words. You were all *snick, snick, fuck you bitch,* and wow. Is that what you did to Dr. Allman?"

"The details are different. The mechanics are the same." My mind raced, but without thoughts. It was all a blur of self-directed disbelief.

The bell rang again, and I whirled, ready to stare Isabella down without saying a single word to her, while I called the police to deal with a trespasser.

My brain crumbled into a pile of wordless ooze

when I saw Joystick and Eli standing on my stoop instead.

Joystick somehow managed to smile in a way that was both sweet and promised so many sinful things. "Hey. Missed you."

"Me too." Eli grasped my fingertips and kissed the back of my hand.

What?

Joystick rested his palm on the side of my face and brushed his lips over mine. The touch was so soft, so barely there, that I reached for the sensation when it was gone, needing just a hint more.

"How do you lead with that? That's not fair." Eli's protest yanked the threads loose that had stalled the gears in my brain.

Joystick looked confused. "You kissed her fucking hand. Why am I the one in the wrong?"

"A kiss like yours melts a person's brain. Look, you broke her." Eli gestured at me.

"I'm not broken." My vocal cords spit out the words before my brain finished processing them.

I wasn't, was I? Not that I ever thought of myself as broken, but for as long I'd pulled away from admitting I was worthy of more than the basics, I might be. "What are you doing here?"

"You didn't answer our messages," Joystick said.

Eli nodded. "We were worried about you. And was that Isabella we saw tearing out of your parking lot?"

"Yeah. Short story, but not worth reliving." Maybe later. Not now.

"Regardless, we missed you," Joystick added. "It's hard to say I love you if the person you want to say it to won't call you back."

"I love you too. I didn't think we were leading with that, but it is why we're here," Eli said.

Was I going to let affection, actual, honest-to-God sweet words, stall me where that woman hadn't? Apparently so.

No. I could handle this. "You should come inside." I opened the door wider.

"I'm gonna go." Lucas kissed me on the cheek. "I want details, but not the gross ones, when you all are done." He walked out and closed the door behind him, locking me in with Eli and Joystick.

They said they loved me. Now that my thoughts were flowing again, the words made my heart sing. Could I—

Lucas's words echoed in my mind. Maybe I would be all right if I did … Could I do this for me? Let myself love and be loved? It was only one thing, but it was a big, terrifying, amazing thing. The kind of thing some people spent their entire lives chasing, and it had fallen into my lap. Twice at almost the same time.

"Kandace," Eli's gentle voice drew my attention, and I met his gaze. "Talk to us. Do you want us to leave? Promise you're all right, and we'll give you whatever you want."

"An entire weekend of incredible orgasms. I make

incredible blueberry pancakes. We could make blue-berry Kandace," Joystick said. "Whatever you want."

What did I want? "I want both of you." That wasn't what I meant to say. But wasn't it? "I want good things, and you're both very good for me, and I love you too, each of you." Was it okay to say that? To even want that?

Lucas was right—I wouldn't hurt anyone who cared about me by doing this. A lifetime of doing otherwise rebelled at the thought of doing something for me, but I really did want this—them.

"Good." Joystick grinned. "Because we might have had to sex-torture you to get you to admit that otherwise."

Eli sighed. "He's kidding. We would never—"

"Unless you begged."

Eli twisted his mouth at Joystick's words. "He's got a point. Seeing you beg to be tied up and given orgasms sounds pretty hot."

My laugh slipped out at their banter. A few weeks ago when I met them, they never would've been like this. We'd all changed, and it was for the better. I refused to slide into mute-Kandace-mode again by being stuck in the fantasy of what they were suggest-ing. I couldn't give them up. Not ever. "What now?"

"Anything you want," Eli said. "We meant that." He gripped the back of my neck, stealing my atten-tion and breath, and crushed his mouth to mine. There was a demand and spark there, the same one that drew me to him the first time we kissed, but stronger. More all-consuming.

What I wanted was to fall into this for a long time. Eli pressed his forehead to mine. "I really did miss you. And I love you so much." His words were soft, but I heard them like the loudest proclamation.

"I love you too."

Joystick dropped to the couch, grasped my hand, and tugged me. I squealed in surprise as he managed to make me lose my balance, and I found myself in his lap.

"Me too." Joystick wrapped an arm around my waist and held me in place. He brushed a few stray strands of hair from my forehead. "Don't forget me. I said it first."

"I could never forget you."

Joystick grinned. "I know." His kiss was harder. Sloppier. And in every way, just as delicious as Eli's.

This was amazing. It might take a while to convince all of me that it was okay, but I was going to. How was I supposed to ignore what these men did to my heart? My mind?

I had an incredible chance before me—beneath me —and I'd be an idiot to let it go. I was going to enjoy this chance—this love—for all I was worth.

30
elijah

I COULDN'T BELIEVE this was my life. I spent so many years quietly resenting Austin. Hating that he got to pick his path and I was forced into mine.

But I wouldn't have enjoyed heading in that direction. I was fucking good at what I did, and I liked it. Though I hadn't picked this to begin with, I wouldn't give it up. I wouldn't surrender having him back in my life, either.

And Kandace...

I could write poetry about Kandace. Long intricate prose about how it felt to be kissing her, right now. To feel her heat. To know that days and weeks and months stretched ahead of us where I got to explore her mind and her body.

This was the kind of ending that wouldn't go in a movie, because no one would believe it, and because this wasn't an end, it was a beginning.

And this was my chance to show them both how

serious I was about them, starting by spoiling Kandace in the bedroom. Maybe at the same time tease Aus— Joystick and show him watching could be fun too.

"Let us show you an incredible day." I tugged Kandace to her feet.

She looked down at herself. "Are you sure you want to be seen in public with someone this frumpy?"

Joystick grasped my hand and I helped him stand as well. He kissed her on the cheek. The neck. The ear. "You're not frumpy in any way," he said.

"You're gorgeous. Through and through." I brushed my lips over hers. "But I don't want to share you with the public today. I'd rather keep you to ourselves for at least a few hours."

With each touch from Joystick or me her body relaxed more. Her sighs became softer and more frequent. "Hmm… no arguments here." Her reply was breathy.

"We should move this into the bedroom." Living room sex was fun and spontaneous, but it wasn't the most comfortable. Besides, Joystick should be sitting somewhere he could prop his leg up.

Kandace led us into her room, and after she moved a few pillows aside, Joystick settled on her bed, his back against the headboard. He grasped her fingers before she could walk away. "You have to stay close, so I can stay hands-on."

I took Kandace's other hand and tangled my fingers with hers. "She's the star of the show. Backstage visit doesn't happen first." I tugged her gently, and pulled her from his grasp.

"When you're right, you're right," Joystick said.

Pink spread across Kandace's cheeks.

I moved the two of us to the middle of the room. When I stripped off my shirt, her gaze fixed on me. I twisted the shirt to turn it into a sort of bandana, and tied it over her eyes as a blindfold.

"I can't see," she protested.

"That's the point." I pressed my lips to the hollow behind her ear. I continued to cover her with kisses as I helped her undress, running my mouth along her back, up her stomach, pausing to suck a nipple into my mouth and tease...

When I had her naked in the middle of the room, I had to step back and admire the beauty in front of me.

She shifted her weight from one foot to the other, and fidgeted with her hands, raising them toward her chest, dropping them near her crotch, as if she was debating which part of herself to cover.

I captured her hands and pissed her palms. "Relax."

"That's easy for you to say. I can't see. I can't do anything."

"You don't need to. This is about your pleasure." I undid my belt and tugged it off in a single zip.

Joystick raised an eyebrow and smirked.

Like that, I understood why he enjoyed having an audience. I loosely bound Kandace's hands behind her back, and led her to a chair near the bed. After positioning it so Joystick would have a good view, I prompted her to sit.

I kissed down her chest, over her stomach, and I knelt to drag my mouth along her inner thighs. When I finally dragged my tongue along her already-wet pussy, I wasn't sure which of us groaned loudest. "You taste so good." I managed the words before devouring her.

The way Kandace squirmed and whimpered under my tongue pushed me to lick harder. Faster. I buried my face between her legs and sucked until she was writhing with each new touch. I drove my tongue inside her, and she arched into my mouth. The sounds she made when I pressed my fingers to her clit were musical.

She clenched around my tongue and wrapped her legs around my body, holding me tight. Riding my face while she let out the most incredible shouts of pleasure. And when she shuddered away, falling back into her seat, my cock was rock hard and wanting its own chance at what I'd just tasted.

I pulled away, and Kandace stilled. Making sure not to make contact with her, I silently rose. I crushed my mouth to hers. Her startled gasp was more fuel on the fire of my need.

She fell into the kiss, biting back. Tasting herself on my mouth. Scooting forward to wrap her legs around me again and press as much of herself into me as possible from her position.

I didn't want to let her go, so I reached up to undo

her blindfold without breaking away. Unbound her wrists.

The moment her hands were free, she grasped the short stands of my hair and pressed into me closer. We clung to each other like we were drowning. Happily. Together.

"You're not going to leave a guy hanging, are you?" Joystick's strained comment wove into the moment.

Kandace and I broke apart, and I couldn't help my chuckle. I turned to see that he'd stripped off his shirt and pushed his jeans down to the top of his legs. His cock was hard and standing at attention, a condom already rolled on.

"Definitely not going to leave you anything but satisfied." Kandace's voice was practically a purr. She moved to the bed on her hands and knees, and crawled toward him.

What an incredible fucking view.

Kandace straddled his legs, and hovered over his erection. I could feel his anticipation. *Feel* her heat, though I was at a distance.

He gripped her and thrust his hips up as he pulled hers down. Her sigh… His grunt…

So good.

I watched for a moment while she set a slow, steady pace, riding Joystick. They were sexy together, no doubt about it, but I wanted to be a part of things.

I knelt behind Kandace and teased my fingers between her legs. Along her opening. Around his cock. I slipped over both until I was inside her. "Lean into Joystick." I kissed her shoulder.

Kandace complied without hesitation, and Joystick rested his hands at the small of her back to hold her.

I took my time stretching her out, relishing both of their reactions. "Do you think you can handle me in there?" I asked Kandace.

"With him?" The catch in her question was delicious. "I want to try."

Me too. I pressed my shaft to his. Good thing she was so slick. So sloppy wet. One agonizing inch at a time, I slipped deeper, until I was buried inside Kandace, my cock resting against Joystick's.

It was tight. Almost too much so. It was *good*.

As we worked our way toward an awkward but eventual rhythm, I traced circles around her clit again. She clenched with each touch, milking me. Making Joystick grunt.

And when we reached a steady pace, I worked her swollen button harder. Faster. When she came again, the way she milked my cock, the pressure, was on the cusp of uncomfortable, and I never wanted it to end.

My mind blanked. Nothing existed but them. But us. Stars danced behind my eyelids. Pressure built inside, tightening in my balls and making me clench my toes.

I recognized the familiar sound of Joystick coming. The jerk of his body. The way he stalled, and then pounded as hard and as fast as was possible in this position.

My own orgasm seemed just out of reach. Until it was here. It tore from me, stealing my breath. Making me dig my fingers into Kandace's thighs. Draining me in the best possible way.

The position we were in made sure we stopped, but I was reluctant to pull away. This was what happy contentment felt like. This was bliss.

Kandace and I were careful pulling away from Joystick, making sure to not jar his cast. I fetched a washcloth and helped them both clean up before sliding into bed with them.

Joystick pulled Kandace into him, and I faced her, holding her. Watching both of them.

This was the kind of incredible I hadn't dared to dream of since I was a teenager. The sort of happily ever after I'd convinced myself only happened in movies and books.

And it was mine.

It was ours.

It was everything.

31
joystick

LAYING in Kandace's bed with her and Eli, in a room that was so distinctly her, was one of the best feelings I never imagined could exist. This space didn't look like the rest of the house, but like her fiery red SUV, it was clear this space was decorated this way because *she* wanted it.

I wanted to spend a lifetime learning about this woman who decorated her walls with modern art prints that were a combination of vibrant reds and blues and purples, blended with soft yellows. Peaches —the fruit and the color. I wanted to learn more about the person who was both bright and soft and lived in this space.

Eli adjusted his position, sliding his hand to rest on Kandace's stomach and tangle his fingers with mine.

And I needed as much time to get to know him, the man I loved when we were boys. I'd seen a bit of who Eli was now, and that taste was enough to make me crave so much more of him.

"What now?" Eli's voice was muted. Lazy. Perfect.

"As in right this minute, or is that a longer term question?" Kandace asked.

I knew the answer to both. "Right now? We cuddle. We do as little as possible aside from getting to know each other. We spend the day in bed, aside from getting up to fetch whatever takeout we order."

Eli laughed. He should do that more often. "You've got this all figured out."

"Not all of it, but a loose plan is forming," I said. "Long term, we'll spend our nights creating and daydreaming and bringing universes and ideas to life while we sit on the floor eating takeout, because a dinner table won't contain our awesomeness. We'll go to the movies and love the show and hate the show and sit in the back row and make out like we're falling in love for the first time every time. We'll decorate my new restaurant and get more paint on us than the walls. We'll ditch parties to drink wine out of the bottle, and we'll do it all together. All three of us."

Kandace made a noise that was half-light laugh, half-contented sigh. She pressed closer to me, bringing Eli with her. "I like the way you think," she said. "No. I *love* the way you think."

This was perfect. More than perfect. This was forever, and I couldn't have asked for a better path forward, or better people to travel it with.

epilogue - kandace

eight months later

THE SMALL AUDITORIUM in the back room of the local bookstore looked quite different tonight than when I'd toured the place with Andrew and Susan—his wife—a month or so ago. Mostly because instead of being empty, several rows of folding chairs were set up facing a large projection screen, and fifty or so of Andrew's closest friends and family.

I was in the front row, between Eli and Joystick, with Lucas and Susan on Eli's other side. As I glanced behind us at the packed makeshift theater, I recognized so many of the faces. Sure, they were here to see the early screener of Andrew's movie, but they were friends of mine, too. People I knew I could call on. People whose company I enjoyed.

I'd spent the last eight months getting used to the kind of love Joystick and Eli showered me with.

Joystick had come out the other side of Isabella's gossip just fine, the way he'd predicted, and through his contacts, Andrew's, and Eli's, we'd heard she couldn't get acting work anywhere.

The time with the men also showed me I'd ignored so much in my life, in order to survive. To make sure Lucas thrived.

Being able to step past that and see there was a life waiting for me that I'd completely overlooked.

I didn't regret the way I'd done things in the past, but I was grateful Eli and Joystick helped me see there was another way to live. Which included picking up the house in Haddarville, and moving in with the men I loved, while Lucas took over my Condo in Salt Lake.

A hush fell over the room as Andrew stood in front of the screen. "Thank you all for coming. Thank you all for living this with me. I hope we've done your memories justice."

With that, he sat next to Susan, and the lights in the room dimmed.

"You all right?" Lucas leaned forward to ask him.

"Sometimes the pictures have to speak for themselves," Andrew said.

That almost sounded wise.

Though I had a good idea what was coming—I'd lived some of it and Eli had been talking about all of it, especially as he helped with last minute edits and re-writes for reshoots. Still, parts of the movie were hard to watch.

Andrew had been through a lot in his life, and some of it was rough. Addiction. Losing friends. The dark side of business—not just because he'd been a founder of the widespread type of internet porn his former company produced.

When some elements got too difficult to consume raw, I focused on finding Eli's influence in the writing. The last several months had given me a great idea of where Eli's logic shone through in most situations, especially over Andrew's compulsion to make the story as extravagant as needed.

As the movie ended, Joystick insisted we pay attention to the credits. Eli's name appeared early on as a co-writer, and according to Joystick, it was important we saw everyone who had worked on the film.

When the house lights rose, it was to a thunderous wave of applause—more noise than I thought a group this size was capable of—that became a standing ovation.

As the clapping and whistles died down, Andrew directed everyone to the banquet room in Gage's, next door. The guests were welcome to eat there or bring their food back here.

Joystick and Gage worked together to cater the event, which Andrew wanted to keep simple and not at all elegant. Joystick insisted on picking up' the tab, as a gift to *his favorite brother-in-law*.

I liked hearing my brother referred to that way, because of what it implied for my relationships.

Joystick's themed bar opened in just a couple of

days, and this was a trial run of sorts for his staff. We'd timed everything to work out this way—the movie, the restaurant opening, all of it. Carly, Raul, and Diego had even flown in.

Apparently just a few weeks ago, when Carly had been traveling for business, she'd run into Isabella mopping floors at a pub in London. Isabella had stammered something, and Carly's response was *I'm just surprised you're capable of honest work.*

I didn't see Carly and her men among the moving crowd scattered with pockets of people who stopped to catch up, but they were here somewhere. They'd left their daughter, Eloise, with Daria for the night. Harmony and Eloise had been so excited for their first ever best friends' sleepover.

Lucas wandered off with Susan, to meet some of the people he'd only ever heard stories about.

Eli, Joystick, and I grabbed some food and found an empty spot in the room to watch. I swore Joystick was more fidgety than normal, glancing around everywhere, not really eating, and not mingling at all.

Was he that nervous about debuting his restaurant's specialty? That didn't seem right.

"Hey, boss lady." Carly's happy greeting cut through my thoughts. She joined us, along with Raul and Diego, and everyone exchanged hugs and handshakes.

"*Man* your childhood was fucked up," Carly said. "And yet, you turned out awesome."

Raul nodded at her. "What she said."

Diego shook his head with his lips pursed. "The movie was very well done, and I have even more respect for you now."

"Thank you." I wasn't sure what to say to any of that.

They drifted away to talk to other people, and I stepped back to watch the crowds. I was so happy for Andrew and the reception this was getting. Eli, for doing such an incredible job bringing it to life. For Joystick and the compliments his food was getting.

And overall I just loved watching all of this with the men I loved by my side.

Andrew let out a loud whistle, and most everyone turned to where he stood to the side of the food tables. "I won't talk long—weird for me, I know, but I promise to let you all go back to your food soon," he said. "Thank you, everyone, for coming. For your support over the years. Your friendship. Everything. But a single person in this room deserves more thanks than anyone else."

Who? I looked around me, as others did the same.

"Kandace." Did Andrew just say my name? "Join me for a minute?"

What?

I was still processing as Joystick nudged me in Andrew's direction, to a round of applause. When I reached my brother, he pulled me into a hug.

"Thank you," Andrew said loud enough for the whole room to hear. "For making sure I survived childhood. For being the best big sister-slash-substitute-mother a kid could have. You never should've had to do that, and you did. Without question. You deserve the best things in this world."

Heat flooded my cheeks, and words escaped me.

He leaned closer and murmured, "you don't have to reply. Just enjoy the gratitude." His words blended with another round of applause.

I tried to be graceful about smiling and taking the congrats, but was happy to return to my men as the attention shifted from me again. The next few hours passed in a blur of catching up,

As the night wound down, and more people had gone than remained, we decided to be on our way as well. We stepped out onto a street that was quiet and dark, in sharp contrast to the room we'd left behind.

We headed toward home—Joystick took the chance to walk everywhere now that his ankle was better—and I was surprised when he steered us toward the door of his dark restaurant.

"Just a quick detour," Eli said.

Okay…

Joystick unlocked the place and let us in. All of the cooking had happened earlier and the clean-up was on the screening site, so it was quiet in here.

Without warning, a faint glow started a few yards away and grew brighter, until one of the tables was lit up with electric candles. Three chairs were placed around it, and a glass dessert dish with fresh berries and cream sat in the middle.

"What is this?" There was a thump-thump in my chest, but I didn't dare make assumptions.

Eli and Joystick both fell to one knee in front of me.

Oh. Oh my.

"Eli wrote this, but I made him let me say it." Joystick grasped the fingertips of my right hand, while Eli took my left.

A nervous laugh escaped my chest. I could almost picture that conversation.

Eli squeezed my hand. "Joystick wanted to do this at the premier, and Andrew agreed, but I told them you didn't want that. This is about us. Only us"

"My life—our lives—changed forever the first time I saw you. The first time I talked to you. Heard you laugh. Tasted your kisses. We don't want to—can't—go back to life without you," Joystick said.

Was he…? Were they…?

"Marry us," Eli added.

My knees were weak. The room swayed.

"Those were my lines," Joystick hissed.

Eli shrugged. "Who knew being quiet could be so hard?"

"Me." Joystick looked at me again, and so did Eli.

"Marry us?" They said in unison.

My legs didn't work. I was too stunned. Too happy. And I was on my knees too. "Yes." That was what I was supposed to say. And *God* it felt good. "Yes, of course yes." Forget good, it felt fucking incredible. "Always and forever, yes."

And then they were kissing me. Joystick cradled my face in his hands and nipped my lips. Eli stole me away to devour my mouth.

Through it all, I laughed, I sighed, I was pretty sure tears were flowing, I was so happy. It all fell between more kisses.

"Wait. Andrew knew?" The rest of my brain caught up, but I refused to be too distracted from the moment.

Eli caught my earlobe between his teeth and tugged before letting go. "Joystick wanted to be proper and ask permission for your hand."

That was both sweet and annoying. "What if Andrew said *no*?"

"I would've decked him and done it anyway." Joystick made it sound like the only reasonable answer. "But I was trying to be appropriate and respectable."

I was laughing again. "Don't. Never do that again."

"Do what?" Joystick asked.

"Be appropriate and respectable. That's not what she loves you for." Eli knew exactly what I was thinking.

"What he just said." I voiced my agreement.

Joystick tried to pout, but he was grinning too hard. Kissing me again and again. "Cross my heart," he murmured.

This was perfect. Wonderful. Better than I thought

I'd deserved, for the longest time. And it was something I'd never give up, no matter what.

———

THANK YOU FOR READING KANDACE, Eli, and Joystick's story.

If you're looking for Andrew and Susan's story, check out RESTRAINT. He runs one of the biggest internet porn companies in the world. She's his best friend's little sister... and a Virgin. He promised to keep his distance, but she's a sweetness he just can't resist.

———

IF YOU LOVE the people you met in Haddarville, I have another series featuring some small town poly romance.

Onyx (along with Alys and Maddox) open the Third and Main series, with DEV GIRL.

Alys has wanted more than friendship from her best friends for years, but men like them don't go for women like her—the shy, dorky dev girl they see as one of the guys.

Onyx suggests a road trip with the three of them, to get their friendship back to where it used to be.

Two weeks driving cross country with her two favorite people? She's going, and she's bringing her master plan to seduce them both.

But the confined quarters and long hours together reveal deeper, darker secrets than how much Alys wants the guys, and by the time the trip is over they may not even have friendship, let alone something more.